WALKING WITH
JESUS

R. A. GILMORE

ISBN: 979-8-9872766-5-5

Table of Contents

Preface

God is the inspiration for the writing of the poems, with the delightful and gracious Holy Spirit leading the process. Learning to be patient and yielding to the Holy Spirit's leading is a joyfully blessed and challenging adventure of growing in faith. The Lord has encouraged and guided this opportunity to work with Him. His hand provides what results as these writings.

The scriptures cited are from the New American Standard Bible, copyright 1971, 1995, 2020. Some other translations are used occasionally and those translations are cited when used.

Though I put the pen to the paper, the pen is guided by the Holy Spirit working through me. I bear the responsibility for the written words and accept the burden of any and all errors. All the honor and glory is to go to God.

I trust this collection of poems will be helpful to the reader and will be an enjoyable venture that draws you closer to God as you walk with the Lord. Perhaps some will provide new insights into your understanding of God's written Word.

God is the poet,
I am the recording secretary.

R. A. Gilmore

Foreword

In every generation, God raises up voices that speak not only with eloquence, but with anointing—voices that echo with timeless wisdom, vibrant faith, and the unmistakable presence of the Holy Spirit. **Dick Gilmore** is one of those voices.

A man seasoned by time yet **young at heart**, Dick writes with a rare combination of spiritual depth and a **zest for life** that is both refreshing and contagious. His poetry is not just the product of talent, but the overflow of a life that has walked closely with God—a life marked by prayer, reflection, and unwavering faith. Each line reveals a heart that is tender, wise, and joyfully **inspired** by the Spirit.

These poems carry the weight of a man who has seen much, endured much, and yet continues to see beauty and hope in the ordinary moments of life. There is **wisdom** here—hard-won and humbly offered.

May his words bless you as they have blessed so many.

Beverly Robinson
Family Pastor,
Grace Place Church

Introduction

Throughout Scripture, we find God is seeking a relationship with people. It starts with God creating people then walking in the garden with Adam. Adam lacked obedience and it cost him his privileged station with God. Others walked with God and enjoyed great fellowship and blessings. Two examples are Enoch and Elijah. Enoch walked with God (Genesis 5:24) and Elijah was one who served God. Elijah did according to the Words of God, performing miracles (1 Kings 17:5). Elijah was transported to heaven in a whirlwind and a fiery chariot (2 Kings 2:11).

One thing about Enoch and Elijah is that each was obedient to God's commands. Walking with God or Jesus requires obedience and Abraham is example one. Abraham's story is found in Genesis 11:27-25:11. It is summarized in Hebrews 11:8-17.

This gives us two parameters for walking with God: obedience and obeying God's commands. What else do we need to be effective in our walk with God/Jesus? As sinful people we must approach God in a way that shows our sincerity in wanting to be with Him. God provided this path (Deuteronomy 4:29; Jeremiah 29:13-14). This path requires us to repent, confess our waywardness, submit to His commandments, then we can be restored to fellowship. "If you seek Me with all your heart, I will be found by you." (Deuteronomy 4:29; Jeremiah 29:13-14).

To Walk with God, we must keep Christ as the center of our life. Christ is the focus of everything we do, say, and think. This includes our relationships, our finances, and our plans. One caution here is that we must remember that we are not perfect. We can strive for perfection but that state will not happen until we sit at Jesus' feet in heaven.

The Benedictine vows to walking with God are stability, obedience, conversion of life, hospitality. Some of the hindrances to walking with Christ are fear, distraction, self-centeredness, lack of faith.

Be sure you are walking *with* and not walking *for* God. Walking *for* God means you are trying to impress Him and you do good things so He will enjoy you. Walking *with* God, you find where He is working and then you work with Him.

There are probably three crucial qualities God is expecting from you: humility, faithfulness and loyalty. We should not try to second-guess God and we should not judge His ways. Remember, God's ways are higher than our ways. (Isaiah 55:8-9).

One thing about walking with God is how does He perceive us? When Christ called the twelve, He used a two- (or 3) word call: (come) follow Me. That call occurs 62 times in the New Testament. When Christ made that simple call, the recipients didn't hesitate and did not ask questions. They left what they were doing and immediately followed Him. Christ was not asking them to take a jaunt with Him from the Sea of Galilee to Bethany. Christ did not call the twelve for a physical experience in walking. In those days, walking was the main form of transportation. Christ called them to forsake all and suffer the consequences, whatever those consequences would be. With their leaving all to follow, they were also called to learning. While it is evident that many (if not each) were having a difficult time with learning, that learning came to full reality at Pentecost. Our following and learning will take time and perseverance on our part and on the part of Christ and the Holy Spirit.

Another facet of Christ's call is that each is called to be a servant (1 Corinthians 3:5 and 4:1). Servants provide service. For an insightful presentation about service and being a servant, see Richard Foster's book *Celebration of Discipline* (3rd edition. Harper San Francisco, 1998) especially the chapter on service. The call to service is amply presented in the New Testament. You can get a glimpse of the concept of service in Matthew 10:1; Romans 12: 1 ff; Romans 15:31; I Corinthians 16:9; 2 Corinthians 9:12; Ephesians 6:6-7; and Hebrews 12:28.

The next critical facet about walking with Jesus is expressing our gratitude and thanks.

If we receive and don't give thanks, we cast aspersions against Christ. Christ is our provider and He is deserving of our giving Him thanks. We freely receive abundant blessings and thus we have the responsibility to offer thanks to the provider.

About half of the books of the Bible have a phrase about giving thanks. Giving honor where honor is due renders our thanks to acclaim our appreciation for what the Lord has done. Giving thanks is a commandment as demonstrated in 1 Thessalonians 5:18, Ephesians 5:20, and Psalm 9:1.

This tome will not be an answer to all your questions and concerns about walking with Christ and living through that adventure. It will provide you a challenge and can lead you to remarkable blessings.

Now it is time for you to begin the journey. Jump in, the water is fine and the blessings are heavenly.

Walk With Jesus

Walk with Jesus along His way
Is the best way to start a day.
He'll never let you go astray
If to Him you fervently pray.

For you He knows the proper road
That will get you to His abode.
On the way, He'll lighten your load,
He'll push you but not with a goad.

Your dragons He will ever slay,
Turn mornings to light from the gray.
He will care for you, come what may,
If we will heed what He does say.

(Written at the Donelson-Hermitage YMCA)

I Come

Lord, I come to You in the morn,
To seek Your guidance for the day,
So I can order all my tasks
And keep me focused on Your way.

Lord, I come to You when it's noon
To give You thanks for what I've done,
To seek forgiveness for my sin
And bask in vic'tries You have won.

Lord, I come when it's even-tide
To review what I've done this day,
To seek forgiveness and give thanks
You held me so I wouldn't stray.

Lord, I come to You at night-time
To pray for family and friends,
To seek healing for those infirm,
To give me rest as this day ends,

(Written at the Donelson-Hermitage YMCA)

Permeation

As I engage the path of life,
Toils, trials are what I see.
Most of that is my perspective
As I am focused just on me.

Change the focus from me to God
And life presents a diff'rent view.
All doubt and dire have been replaced
With a love that's gracious and true.

Walking with God, with hand in hand,
Joy does permeate through my soul.
Much can be accomplished each day
As long as it's God I extol.

(Written at the Donelson-Hermitage YMCA)

Living

My soul does long for God's leading
And how do I assuage my thirst,
To keep my heart from being parched?
With intention I put God first.

My very being God does feed
With the sweet manna of His Word.
As long as God's first in my thought
Then His orations will be heard.

My existence becomes living
Because God's ever in control.
His love and mercy o'er me flows
And ever Him I will extol.

(Written at the Donelson-Hermitage YMCA)

Follow

We've been gifted with a new day.
The first thing is take time to pray,
Asking God to show us His way,
That through my life, God's on display.

As I'm about the daily task,
Doing whatever God does ask,
God, help me to shed my me mask
So that in Your love I can bask.

When ev'ning comes and time to rest
I pray that I have done my best
To live my life full of Your zest
And followed You as my life's quest.

(Written at the Donelson-Hermitage YMCA)

The Christ

O gracious Love that won't let go
Draw me ever closer to Thee.
Break asunder the bonds I've set
So that in You I will be free.

Remove the blinders from my eyes
So that it's You that I can see.
Grace me with a white robe of love
So ever I'll belong to Thee.

Use me for Your great purposes
So that in me Your will be done.
Not that I would be lifted up,
But for Christ each day would be won.

(Written at Grace Place Church)

Life Style

We've a guide for each step we take
But do we yield to that guidance?
Are we our own guide for our life
And with us do we freely dance?

Christ wants to be an active part
Of our life, life that He did give.
Christ wants what's best for each of us,
Abundant life for us to live.

Commit your life to live for Christ
And to follow what He has planned.
A life fully yielded to Christ
Is a life that is full and grand.

(Written at Grace Place Church)

The Prize

It's not the swiftness of your trek,
It is the slow and steady pace
That gets you to the finish line
With a sweet smile upon your face.

Perseverance will get you through
The hills and vales of your life's way.
One other thing that you will need
Is consistence in prayer each day.

Prayer's the foundation of each day
Upon which to build as you rise.
Remember that in all you do
Eternal life with Christ's the prize.

(Written at the Donelson-Hermitage YMCA)

Called

We are called to be good neighbors.
We are called to be salt and light.
We are called to study God's Word.
We are called to bring love, do right.

We are called to do God's justice.
We're called to do mercy for God.
We're called to walk with God humbly.
We're called to witness where we trod.

We are called to be God's servants.
We are called to persecution.
We are called to be prayer warriors.
We're called to be God's reflection.

Christ's Plan

As I traverse the path of life
God's Spirit oft takes me to task,
Make me to pause, to think things through
And encouraging me to ask.
Questions come tumbling from my mind
Refocusing so I can be sure
That I'll be doing the right thing
And in Christ's love I'll be secure.
Such guidance does come from the Lord
Lights my path, shows me the right way,
Keeps me ever within Christ's plan
So in His love I'll ever stay.

God's Requirement

With what shall I come to the Lord
And bow before the God on high?
Does He require burnt offerings
And bleating of sheep as they cry?

In what does the Lord take pleasure,
Thousands of rams, rivers of oil?
For my sins what can I provide
Thousands of hours of my toil?

The Lord has told you what is good
And what He does require of you.
To do justice and love kindness,
Walk humbly with God, you're to do.

(Micah 6:6-8)

Full Life

It's a new day, how did you start?
Did God hold first place in your heart?
Your agenda rest of the day,
Is God involved in all you say?

When do you read God's holy Word?
When is it, from you, God has heard?
Do you, each day, take time to play?
Do you, each day, take time to pray?

Is God involved in all your life,
The good, the bad and even strife?
For a full life, we need God's way,
So we must seek what He would say.

(Written at the Donelson-Hermitage YMCA)

Reflect

Life does confront us ev'ry hour,
Many decisions we must make.
Some decisions we make in haste,
For others, much time we do take.

What's our guiding purpose in life?
How do we use it in each step?
Is it just a mantra we speak
Or does it our life give some pep?

Do we intentionally seek
The Lord to guide away from strife?
Do we seek God to guide our way
So we reflect Christ's love in life?

(Written at Grace Place Church)

God's Best

Our life is so full of questions,
Answers we want are hard to find.
Some answers are available,
These answers are not the right kind.

Are we going to let us yield,
The expedient thing to do?
Do we have the patience to wait
And let God's answers see us through?

God's answers are always the best,
Only God knows the blessed way.
Take a deep breath, relax and wait
So we can be God's best today.

(Written while visiting Marilyn and Tom Dumm in
Naples, FL)

Living Life

Life comes so furious and fast.
We have but one life we can live.
It's not about what you can get,
It's all about what you do give.

Slow down and look at what you do.
Is self where your attention goes?
Is your emphasis about you?
What is it that your action shows?

When you make plans for what to do,
The only way to truly live,
And make a life that is worthwhile,
Based on how much of you, you give.

(Written at the Donelson-Hermitage YMCA)

Serve

How do you effectively serve
Others in your community?
So many avenues are there
And most of these we do not see.

Non-profits always seek for help,
Elderly neighbors need a hand.
You can always be a mentor,
A smile, kind words are always grand.

We seem to not have enough time
Yet use of time's in our control.
Serve others first and you will find
That time will bless your heart and soul.

Good Deed

It is a new year, time to start
New ways and things within your life.
The first best thing to bring about
Is to reduce stress in your life.

Change your focus from you to them.
What can you do to help others.
It's always good to remember
That we're all sisters and brothers.

One way to serve is a good deed
That you provide and they don't know
Who it was that did that nice thing.
Then let only your heart to glow.

The Christ

O Christ, the Savior of my soul,
Help me to put You in control.
Help me to yield my all to You,
May You shine through all I do.

Forgive me, get me on Your way,
Let me be wholly Thine each day.
My heart, soul, spirit I commend
To You my precious, faithful friend.

May each of my words honor You.
May my actions honor You too.
May all my being lift You up
And then, O Lord, please fill my cup.

(Written while at lunch at a restaurant)

Life

The Rock is a firm foundation,
A stronghold and a sure defense,
A cleft of refuge in danger
And for sinners, our recompense.

Upon that Rock we safely build
A life that's kind and full of love.
A life that's light in the darkness,
A life centered on Him above.

A life that's built upon the Rock
Will persevere through struggles, strife.
That life will bring honor, glory
To the One that's the source of life.

(Written at the Donelson-Hermitage YMCA)

Prayer

Lord Jesus hear us as we pray,
Seeking Your guidance for the day.
Whether it's work or even play
Help us to find Your perfect way.

No matter what it is we do,
Please keep us ever close to You.
Help us be strong and carry through,
Yielding to what You do imbue.

Lord Your witness may we be,
It's only in You that we're free.
For fulness of life You're the key.
May others in us You they'll see.

(Written at the Donelson-Hermitage YMCA)

Commandment

Christ gave them a new commandment,
It's that you love one another.
From the world's perspective, it's strange
And the world would say why bother.

Honoring that commandment now
Would impact the way that we live.
No more rancor be the lead,
No more malice, just love we'd give.

That commandment's a way of life
That's sorely needed e'en today.
Lord Jesus please change all our hearts
So that now we would live Your way.

(Written at Grace Place Church)

Life

He was young, smart and he knew it.
His good looks would carry him far.
He held his head high, and did strut.
For him, he was his leading star.

He was self-made, or so he thought,
He still had very much to learn.
His world did crumble all around
'Fore his eyes he did crash and burn.

Real life was now before his eyes,
He saw there was a choice to make.
His self-image had let him down.
With the choice, which one would he take?

Yielding to God's Holy Spirit,
On his knees he confessed his sin,
Accepted Christ as his Savior,
New life in Christ then he did begin.

Now a humble witness for Christ,
All to Christ he does freely give.
He emptied himself at Christ's feet,
Now it's for Christ that he does live.

(Written at the Donelson-Hermitage YMCA)

Seen

Lord Jesus come and cleanse my heart
And while You're at it, cleanse my mind.
Make every part of me clean,
Then with Your love, all of me bind.

Remove each iota of dross,
Take away each and ev'ry sin.
Put holy sound plugs in my ears
So I won't hear all the world's din.

Scrub me with Your heavenly soap,
Purge me with hyssop, make me clean.
Prepare me as Your sacrifice
So that in me it's You that's seen.

(Written at Grace Place Church)

Intent

Jesus, to Thee I humbly come,
My sinful self I give to You.
If I control, life goes awry.
I don't know why, can't find a clue.

Your servant's what I want to be.
Please use me as Your instrument.
You alone should be lifted up
And as for me, that's my intent.

Shake me hard as a dirty rag
That all my dross be cast away.
Clothe me in Your sweet righteousness,
Hold me tight so that I don't stray.

(Written at Grace Place Church)

Provisions

God is my strength and my refuge,
He is the cleft, a safe hiding place.
He is my stronghold, sure defense,
He's my provider, He gives grace.

When troubles arise, He is there
To guide, direct and show the way.
He intercedes on my behalf,
When I can't, He will always pray.

God's my comforter, assurance.
In Him I can ever find rest.
He's always there and always right.
For my life He knows what is best.

(Written at Grace Place Church)

Pray

Lord, we try and often we fail.
We persevere and it's for naught.
We try to correct errant ways
And review all that we've been taught.

We pray and wonder, does God hear?
Am I really that far off track?
Did I miss a lesson or two?
Just what is it that I do lack?

Growth only occurs by trying.
Success will come, but in God's way.
We are to do, not to keep score,
Persevere, continue to pray.

(Written at the Donelson-Hermitage YMCA)

Me

I need to be the one true me,
But who's the me I want to be?
A different me in each place
Means to change masks for whom I face.

A problem comes, as you do see.
What is the only true one me?
It is a puzzle to unroll
Which of the me's is in control.

Lord, sort me out and set me straight
So true me meets You at the gate.
Please make me one in You O Lord
Let me live by Your Holy Word.

(Written at Grace Place Church)

Values

Mankind's values can not compare
With the values Jesus does share.
Mankind's values fade from the earth,
Jesus' values, eternal worth.

Prestige and honor man does eke,
True service is what Christ does seek.
Mankind seeks for a life of ease
Christ seeks those praying on their knees.

Mankind seeks to be put above,
Christ seeks those of agape love.
Mankind does seek for strength and verve,
Christ seeks those whom others they serve.

All the comparisons do show
Christ's values are the ones to know.
Apply them to the life you face
And seek the Christ's amazing grace.

His Hand

Jesus offers to us His hand
And all we have to do is take.
Take His hand and then hold on tight,
Then us His followers He'll make.

Keeping a tight grip on His hand
Allows Him to guide in His way.
Each time He squeezes our hand tight
Is a signal for us to pray.

When we loosen our grip on Him
Is when we stumble, even fall.
He's right there to catch and lift up
And remind us on Him to call.

(Written at a restaurant while having lunch)

Pursue

I'm blessed by Christ in all I do
If it is Him I do pursue.
Blessings wane when I go my way
So it's with Christ I try to stay.

When my mind's on Him, then I'm up,
He continues to fill my cup.
No matter what I try to do,
He is faithful to follow through.

When the day ends and I do sleep
I know that my soul He will keep.
In the morn when I do awake
He will show me the path to take.

(Written at the Donelson-Hermitage YMCA)

My Keeper

O Lord, I want to follow You,
Be Your servant in all I do.
I need Your help in many ways.
In all my ways may You shine through.

May all my words be gracious, kind,
May all my actions reflect You.
May my thoughts be based on Your love,
May my walk guide others to You.

You're the one to control my life.
Only You can answer my prayer.
Your ways for my life I do seek,
You keep me safe everywhere.

(Written while having lunch at a restaurant)

Leader

Who is the leader of your day?
If it's you, do you go astray?
If a friend, is it one that's right?
If your boss, ever in their sight?

Does your leader encourage you?
And to you is your leader true?
Do you follow that lead each day?
Does your leader call you to pray?

Christ is the leader each does need.
On His Word daily we should feed.
Daily to Christ oft we should pray.
He will never lead you astray.

(Written at the Donelson-Hermitage YMCA)

Leader

He has the plan I'm to follow
To get me to the heav'nly land.
It's not an easy way to go
But He will take me by the hand.

I will stumble along the way,
He'll be right there to lift me up.
When I struggle 'cause of thirst,
From His pitcher He'll fill my cup.

Though I am weak, in Him I'm strong.
When I wander, He'll set me straight.
When I languish and can't go on
He will carry me through the gate.

(Written while at lunch at a restaurant)

The Place To Be

Where do you find a quiet rest,
Where great peace does relax your soul,
Where you let your cares fly away,
And where you are not in control?

Is there a place where you do share
All of the burdens of your heart,
Where neatness is of no concern,
Where love's the one and only part?

There is a one and only place
That you will find where ere you trod.
It is the place to ever be
And that's near to the heart of God.

(Written at Grace Place Church)

See Christ

God be ever present with me.
Open my eyes that I might see.
Open my ears that I may hear
Your gentle words so loud and clear.

Open my mind, Your word to know
That all my life it's You I show.
Have my actions be about love
That show the path to God above.

Let all my life be about You
That through me You come shining true.
Help me to live, not about me,
But that Christ is whom they do see.

(Written at Grace Place Church)

Follow

Always being of good courage
As we walk by faith, not by sight.
Our desire, be pleasing to Christ
And in Christ's eyes, do all things right.

Each will receive our just reward
According to our earthly deeds.
Not so much for reaping harvest,
But based upon our planting seeds.

Our role is to follow Jesus
And His plan for us to fulfill.
If we follow Christ day by day,
Then we are displaying God's will.

(2 Corinthians 5:6-10)
(Written while visiting Beth and Steve Gilmore in
Tucson, AZ)

Gentle Spirit

Be strong in Christ and persevere,
Patiently waiting for His call.
Confirmation He then will give
So that you won't stumble and fall.

Go forth in the strength of the Christ
E'er proclaiming the Word of God.
Some will disdain you, some will hear,
Speak Christ's peace wherever you trod.

You'll be fought, but not overcome,
God is there to deliver you.
Always wear a gentle spirit
So Christ is seen in all you do.

(Jeremiah 1:17-19)
(Written at the home of Kathy and Tom Gilmore in
New Palestine, IN)

Grace

Life unfolds around us each day
With expectations, disarray.
Do we respond or just react?
Does grace prevail with loving tact?

Do grudges hang around our neck
Like a millstone that we do check?
Do we ever keep looking back
To be sure there's no rear attack?

Enjoy life, with punches just roll,
Remember God is in control.
Greet life with a smile on your face
Remember you've been saved by grace.

(Written at Grace Place Church)

Thine

Holy Jesus please hear my plea.
With heart and soul I cry to Thee.
Take this earthen vessel of clay,
Make it what You want it to be.

Cleanse me with fire, don't let me burn.
Whatever I've done is just dross.
Purify me with Your Spirit,
Teach me how to carry my cross.

May all my life glorify You.
Make me strong so I'll never whine.
Help me love others like You do
That always I'd be wholly Thine.

(Written at Grace Place Church)

Foundation

What is the purpose of your life?
Is it for joy, avoiding strife?
What do you see that's for the end
As you turn on that final bend?

Just what will others think of you
When your days on this orb are done?
Is it a path to heav'n you trod
As you prepare to meet your God?

Now is the time, this is the day
For you a foundation to lay
For the eternal life you'll win
Full of guilt or free from all sin.

(Written at Grace Place Church)

Encounter

We encounter a lot in life,
There's trials, troubles, rain and snow.
At the end of each day or year
What good things do we have to show?

We encounter friends and others
And to these how do we respond?
Are we gracious and welcoming
Developing a cordial bond?

What about encountering Christ?
Do we pass Him off as a whim?
Do we pause, reflect on our ways
And surrender our life to Him?

(Written while at lunch at a restaurant)

Shepherd of My Soul

Lord, You're the shepherd of my soul,
It is to You that I belong.
I need Your help, I need Your grace,
It is through You that I am strong.

Take my sinful self in Your arms,
Wash me so that I can be clean.
Inspire my heart, my soul, my mind
That from You about life I'd glean.

Help me to free myself from me
That only on You I'd depend.
Guide all my thoughts and all my ways
So I could truly be Your friend.

(Written while at lunch at a restaurant)

Teach Me

O Lord, please teach me of Thy ways
That more about You I would know.
Expand my mind, expand my heart
That ever in You I would grow.

Your precepts are the key to life
The life that You would have me live.
Grow me so I can bear the fruit,
That fruit then I would freely give.

Be a protective hedge 'round me
So I would not slip and fall.
Ever have me ready for You
To respond to Your beck and call.

(Written while at lunch at a restaurant)

Jesus' Feet

We look about and wonder why
The people do not turn to You.
You are the way, the truth and life,
Your burden's light, that we can do.

You know the way that we should go,
You are the light upon the road,
You are the rock on which to stand,
In You we have a safe abode.

Lord, help us to have more intent,
Often for others to entreat.
Help us to do more, show more love
That more would come to Jesus' feet.

(Written at Grace Place Church)

Mercy and Grace

O Lord, we come on bended knee,
Our sinful selves we do present,
Pleading for others and for us
That on us Your wrath You'll not vent.

Your help we desire and we need
Yet Your help we do not deserve.
Sinful ways do overtake us,
On our plate wrath's what You should serve.

Forgive us we do humbly pray,
Our sinful hearts too well You know.
We don't want to lead sinful lives,
Mercy and grace on us bestow.

(Written at Grace Place Church)

Neighbor

A new commandment Christ did give
That we should love one another.
Set aside all anger and angst,
Love them as sister or brother.

We're also to love our neighbor
And treat them just like family.
Help and serve them along the way,
Make them like a growing lily.

Be there for them at any time,
Don't set them aside on a shelf.
Be proactive in what you do
And love your neighbor as yourself.[1]

---

1. Luke 10:27

Your Call

God has a purpose for each one,
Wants each to be available
To heed the call that He does place
And in His grace to be stable.

It's not too late to start anew
To step out in God's adventure.
God will give you the needed strength
To help you progress and endure.

God's way is always exciting
And He will never let you fall.
Boldly step out to serve the Lord
Take a chance to fulfill your call.

Decision

We're urged to buy, to gather things,
It's those things that happiness brings,
That strum a tune on our heart strings,
Makes us leap as the doorbell rings.

So how does this fit on the page
Along with things that are the rage,
That make us overspend our wage,
And compare it to God's message.

Do we consume the Lord's vision
Or carry out the Lord's mission?
To serve/give is our discretion,
And now what is your decision?

Do, Love, Walk

A sad event has just transpired,
We've been put on proper notice.
Their cry: for justice or revenge?
For God calls us to do justice.

Care for others we all do plead,
The need is there as we can see.
The cry: for mercy or pity?
For God calls us to love mercy.

We walk for leisure and for health,
Sometimes we jog, sometimes we plod.
No matter how we get about
We're to walk humbly with our God.

(Micah 6:8)
(Written at Grace Place Church)

A Quiet Place

A quiet place, a time alone
With no TV, no telephone,
A time with God where I can hear
That still strong voice so calm and clear.

A quiet place, no distractions,
Where God's light gives great refractions.
Pushing away all other thought,
It's where I ponder what God's taught.

That is where I begin each day
As to and with God I do pray,
Seeking help and the will of God
Before upon His earth I trod.

(Written at Grace Place Church)

Views

We travel the roads to get there
Wherever it is "there" will be.
In this context of our going
We claim that it has set us free.

With all of this moving about
Just what is our destination?
It's not about a local jaunt,
It's all about our salvation.

With all of this constant moving
How do we ever settle in?
Do we ever find or take time
For our eternal life to win?

All we do should be Christ-centered,
Ready to proclaim Christ's good news.
Then each of our moving about
Will provide us heavenly views.

(Written at Grace Place Church)

Living In Him

In the stillness of the night
The still small voice sets us right.
There's no need for us to fight,
Of the world, He is the light.

In the calmness of the day
Is when oft we go astray.
Yet it's with Him we should stay
For He has the proper way.

In the midst of life's trials
We're burdened with times dials.
We forget we need smiles,
We'll walk with Him for miles.

Living Life

We build walls that are strong and tall.
We think it helps keep others out.
Yet all it does is keep us in
Where alone we can brood and pout.

Include some others not like you
And cast your vision far and wide.
You can do this, give it a try,
Ask one to join you at your side.

Be a blessing to one and all,
Offer your help to one in need.
Ask for advice from some others.
Be careful what advice you heed.

Do an anonymous good deed
And try to do it once each week.
Help bear the burdens of others.
Be intentional as you seek.

You are not perfect, no one is.
See something needing done, do it.
If not successful, try again.
What you try first just may not fit.

You cannot judge others motives.
Learn from mistakes and grow from there.
Be certain that in all you do
You invite some others to share.

Grow

For our plants, we take proper care
With water, fertilizer, sun.
We do provide them special love
Until the growing season's done.

Our spiritual growth needs our care
With water, fertilizer, sun.
We need to be watered with prayers,
Fed with God's Word so we can run.

We need Son shine from the Spirit
To allow our spirit to grow.
We need to be laved with God's love
Until the Lord we truly know.

Our growing season's never done
Cultivation needs good content.
From our first cry, our spirit grows
But only with proper intent.

Our nurturing never does cease,
From age to age it must go on.
Proper purpose must lead the way
Until eternal life is won.

Dross

We live in a world that is wild
And we long for a life that is mild.
Information overload's there,
It's more like a life of despair.

Electronically we're besieged
We wonder if its ill-conceived.
Facebook postings, twitter and tweets
Texts and snap chat are not my sweets.

Post-it notes are everywhere,
TV ads too often do blare.
Vehicle traffic's way too much
With autos, bikes, scooters and such.

Pan- and endemics ev'rywhere,
Each giving a medical scare.
Masks to be worn upon the face.
Social distancing's a disgrace.

High inflation's getting us down,
In abundant new laws we drown.
There's only one place for this dross
And that's at the foot of the cross.

God's Calling

God stretches forth His trusting hand
Inviting each to join His way.
His love for us will never sway,
His plan for us is ever grand.

God's way is not an easy go,
Perseverance we'll ever need
As on His Word we daily feed.
On His path, step by step He'll show.

Yield to God's calling on your life,
It is a life that's ever full.
Very few moments will be dull
And you will not be free of strife.

In this life you will quickly find
Abundant blessings come your way.
You'll find fulfillment as you pray
And you will have great peace of mind.

Love

Love is the essence of our life,
Love your friends and enemies too,
And love your neighbor as yourself,
Let love pour out in all you do.

Love all those who show you spite,
Even love those who you they shun.
Love all those who have done you wrong,
Love those who even from you run.

Love those who ail and those infirm,
Love those who have been sent to jail.
Love the elderly and the sick,
Love all the children without fail.

(Written while sitting in the dining room lobby at
the Terrace Hotel at Lake Junaluska, NC)

The Sword

Only he who heartily drinks
From the well of eternal Word
Is the one who remains healthy
And thus able to serve the Lord.

Only he who believes abides.
Abiding in Christ makes life new,
Life that is abundant and free,
Life that reflects Christ in full view.

Only he who follows Jesus
Will be the one who conquers fear.
Follow Christ's footsteps and His way
If Christ's Words you expect to hear.

Only he who knows you dearly
Purchased you and me and others,
Sees in his neighbor the Savior,
Has compassion on his brothers.

Do we understand in all its
Intensity Christ's Holy Word?
It's our starting point to regain
Health and wholeness to serve the Lord.

It's not the sword of Damocles
That ever hangs over our head.
It is the sword of Jesus Word
And that's on what we should be fed.

Christ's tears are ever being shed
All over our iniquity.
His Word will never satisfy
Until we dive ever deeply.

(Based on Helmut Thielicke's book *How the World Began*, pages 216-217)

Trust in God

Open your heart unto the Lord,
Harken unto His Holy Word.
Ever seek His guidance for you,
So you'll prosper in all you do.

Prayer's your communication route,
Through prayer you can resolve your doubt.
With prayer your faith can truly grow,
Through prayer, God you can get to know.

Prayer is two-way conversation,
Heart to heart, no reservation.
Plead and listen go hand-in-hand,
Trust in God, He will understand.

(Written while on the porch of the Terrace Hotel at
Lake Junaluska, NC)

Abide

It's in God's Word I put my hope
In addition, God is my stay.
Hold firmly, He's the Word of life,
He'll never let you go astray.

Abide in God, that's where you grow,
You can not make it on your own.
You need God, He wants you as His,
Let Him your very life to hone.

Open your heart, let Christ come in,
With Christ make a relationship.
As you are hanging out some day
Hang out with Christ – not a guilt trip.

(Based on Joy Sherman's sermon at Grace Place
Church on May 15, 2022)

Insistent

Humbly receive God's planted Word
For this will ever save your soul.
Don't just sit there and hear the Word
Be doers, that's God in control.

Those who truly follow God's Word
In them God's love's been perfected.
And all who see will surely know
We're one in Christ as directed.

Be steadfast as you wait for God
His Word comes to you in His time.
May those who fear you see the Lord
Wait for His Word, it won't form rime.

(James 1:21-22; 1 John 2:5; Psalm 119:74
(Based on Joy Sherman's sermon at Grace Place
Church on May 15, 2022)

Invested

Do all that's written in God's Word
And your way will be prosperous.
There is no cause to be dismayed
And in God's strength be courageous.

Hold firmly to the Word of life.
As a drink off'ring, be poured out
As a sacrifice of service.
Rejoice and put away all doubt.

The return on your investment?
It will enhance your witness too.
Share the great joy that you receive
As God's Word does carry you through.

(Joshua 1:8; Philippians 2:16)
(Based on Joy Sherman's sermon at Grace Place
Church on May 15, 2022)

Intentional

Have God's Word ever on your heart
Diligently to repeat them
To your children and your fam'ly.
Cherish God's Word, it is a gem.

Let God's Word be first as you talk
And always be first in your mind.
If His Word inhabits your soul
God's comforting peace you will find.

Let God's word inhabit your speech,
Express God's Word in all you do.
Be intentional with God's Word
And that word will carry you through.

(Deuteronomy 6:6-9)
(Based on Joy Sherman's sermon at Grace Place
Church on May 15, 2022)

God's Word

God's Word's the sword of the Spirit
And in residence in our life.
When it's there we are emboldened
And then it can reduce our strife.

We have to get into God's Word
To have God's Word inhabit us.
To put us in a better place
A daily dose will be a plus.

God's Word brings enlightenment
Regardless of our persuasions.
God's Word's bread for daily living
Not cake for special occasions.

(Based on Joy Sherman's sermon at Grace Place
Church on May 15, 2022)

Battles

We face battles throughout our life,
Some are earthly, some heavenly.
For each we need right battle gear
To prepare for fights properly.

God's armor is invincible,
With it all our battles He'll win.
This armor is one size fits all,
It will withstand all of the din.

Carry with you the shield of faith,
Don the helmet of salvation.
Sharpen the sword of the Spirit,
Keep alert with supplication.

(Based on Joy Sherman's sermon at Grace Place
Church on May 15, 2022)

The Path Of Life

Lord, as I walk this path of life
Please take my hand and be my guide.
Get me around the potholes there
And ever stay there at my side.

Keep me from pitfalls on the way.
Keep me from wan'dring off the trail.
Help me stay focused just on You
So that my life I don't derail.

It is a long path to follow,
Diversions occur at each turn.
Please keep me steadfast on Your way
And only You for whom I'd yearn.

(Written while in the exam room waiting for the
doctor)

What Do You Find?

What do you find in your morning walk?
What do you find in fresh morning air?
What do you find in what greets your eye?
What do you find in time of despair?

What do you find as you read God's Word?
What do you find with time spent in prayer?
What do you find as you drive to work?
What do you find in the time you share?

What do you find with the words you speak?
What do you find in meditation?
What do you find as you pause and think?
What do you find in consternation?

What do you find through agitation?
What do you find in others you see?
Through each of these with the grace of God
You'll find the you God wants you to be.

Obey

The Lord does call, and we do hear,
What the Christ asks may not seem right.
We look at reason and our pride
And we want to shrink out of sight.

Following Jesus has a cost,
That cost may cause our life to fray.
God's call is not about debate,
If we follow, we must obey.

Jesus' call is to follow Him
And He will not lead you astray.
There's only one requirement,
It is Jesus you must obey.

Fruit

A gen'ral empathy for all,
Underserved yet sent from the Dove,
Concern for the good of others.
This is the fruit that is named love.

A deep feeling of contentment
That to others you would deploy.
It's your response to outside things
And it's the fruit we know as joy.

Harmony of mind and spirit
E'en when outside things do not cease.
A tranquil state of faith and trust
That comes from God, the fruit of peace.

Persevere through difficulties
Waiting for God in His silence
Shows our relationship with God
Is His form of fruit called patience.

Actions of encouraging words
And integral to our witness
Our hearts are inclined to others
By the gracious fruit of kindness.

Actions that benefit others
And done without any bias
Puts needs of others above ours
Displays the fruit we call goodness.

Fidelity to promises
A gracious trait that is boundless.
Persevering when things seem worst
Displays the fruit of faithfulness.

A strong hand that has a soft touch
Compassion for others' weakness
A humble heart from inward grace
It is God's fruit of gentleness.

Be of sound mind and keep one's head
Are traits each of us should extol.
These reflect the Spirit of God
Also the fruit of self-control.

(Galatians 5:22-23)

God of Grace

O Lord, another day has dawned,
With it new challenges are spawned.
Guide me through the tasks of this day
Keeping me ever on Your way.

My soul and spirit please restore
So I am Yours forevermore.
Renew, restore my faith in You
So You'll be seen in all I do.

Confirm my mind, spirit and heart
So that from You I'll never part.
Confirm my thoughts, make them all Thine
So my words with You will align.

Strengthen my body and my mind
That always Your will I do find.
Strengthen my doing that I'll be
Ever a strong witness for Thee.

Establish me firm in Your will
So that Your precepts I fulfill.
Establish me strong in Your hand
That all the foe's darts I'll withstand.

O Lord please fill me with Your grace
That through this life I will not race.
As You establish me in You
Strengthen me for what I must do.

Through Your grace, confirm and restore
Granting me peace forevermore.
O Lord of all, I'm here, use me
So I'll ever glorify thee.

(1 Peter 5:10)
(Written at Covenant Presbyterian Church,
Nashville, TN)

Leaky

Lord make me a leaky or a cracked pot
That as You pour love and blessings on me
That just on me they would not be
    constrained
But that they'd leak out for others to see.

Lord not only would those blessings be seen
But others would experience them too.
Thus Lord make me so leaky with Your love
That it would seep through ev'rything I do.

Lord as You pour love and healings on me
Let all my leakiness grow bigger still
That as I proceed through all my days
Others would gain insight into Your will.

(Written at the Donelson-Hermitage YMCA)

Self

Lord, we're so self-centered in all our ways
And we think our world revolves around us.
When things go awry and not go our way
We get rattled, shaken and raise a fuss.

You should guide us, yet we inform
    ourselves.
Though You should rule us, we've taken
    control.
Though You can forgive us, we think we're
    free.
Though You should fill us, ourselves we
    console.

We think Your truth's too high, Your will
    too hard,
Your power too remote, Your love too free.
Our perspective is so far out of line
That such miserable people we be.

We need Your Word to heal our confused
   minds.
We need Your law to heal our divided wills.
Troubled consciences need Your healing
   love.
Anxious hearts calm as Your presence
   fulfills.

Lord, reclaim us from our self-centered path.
Extract us from sinful mirey clay.
Purge us and lave us so we can be clean
And then restore us to Your righteous way.

(Written at Covenant Presbyterian Church,
Nashville, TN)

New Life

In your quest for earthly pleasures and the
social ladder part,
Do you find life brings contentment and
satisfaction to your heart?
Do you find yourself still searching for
meaning in all around?
Do you think there's more to life than that
which you've already found?

There's a bright new dimension to this life
here that you lead,
And the way to achieve it is so simple, yet
indeed
It will require complete surrender and then
some effort made by you
To make some changes in your thinking
about everything you do.

Just give all of yourself to Jesus at this
    moment of this day.
Call upon Him now and ask Him to forgive
    you while you pray.
Confess that you're a sinner and brand-new
    life you want to start.
And Pray, not from your mind, but from the
    very bottom of your heart.

On Jesus Christ you can depend from this
    moment evermore.
He will bring such fulfillment like you've
    never had before.
He will bring a new understanding to what
    fuller life can be,
Because He's the only one who from sin can
    set us free.

Pleasing God

What is it that would please the Lord?
Is it sacrifices we bring?
Is it our reading of the Word?
Is it the hymns and songs we sing?

Is it the words that we do speak?
Is it the sacraments we share?
Is it attendance at the church?
Is it the countenance we wear?

None of these will justify us!
In all the ways that we do trod,
We're to do justice, love mercy,
And to walk humbly with our God.

(Micah 6:8)

Life With God

Lord, You have graced us with Your love,
Sent Your angels to minister,
Sent Your Spirit to indwell us,
Claimed us though we were a sinner.

To You we can confess our sin
And forgiveness You do proffer.
You desire us to come to You
And our hearts to You surrender.

Wholly Yours You want us to be
And You'll be our total cleanser.
In Your will You want us immersed
So we can be Your messenger.

(Written while visiting Marilyn and Tom Dumm in
Mayville, NY)

Dancing With God

Dance occurs in several forms.
It could be group, could be solo.
Often it does happen in pairs
And can bring an amazing glow.

Dancing with God is a two-some,
A cooperative task indeed.
One important thing to recall,
In this dance, God always does lead.

It's important to be alert
And receptive to what's around.
With contemplative awareness
We see God in all that's around.

Response is a must for the dance,
It is to obey what we hear.
It is to will God's will for us,
Discerning hearts we should revere.

Free to follow where God does lead
Means detach from culture's values
And ubiquitous tentacles
Of temptation and its taboos.

God's creation we can enjoy
Without owning or destruction.
Appreciate one thing each time
Slowly and without exhaustion.

God desires that we dance with Him
To delight in His partnership,
A time of gracious joy and love
That brings us Edenic worship.

Reflections

My heart and soul tend to wander,
Lord, keep them in Your holy place.
Let my wanderings be to You
And fill me with Your love and grace.

Let my feet follow Your guiding,
Keeping me on Your perfect path.
Help me to ever yield to You
That I might not incur Your wrath.

May I be a good reflector
In ev'rything I say and do,
That my presence would not be seen,
All would see only Christ and You.

(Written at Covenant Presbyterian Church,
Nashville, TN)

Fulfill

What is it that fulfills your life,
The driving force within your heart?
How then does this impact your acts
And the words that you do impart?

It's only God that can fulfill
And in your heart provide the drive
To make you a blessing to all
And make you live, not just to thrive.

The more you do give of yourself,
The more that God will then fulfill.
Blessings will ever come your way
And peace for you God will instill.

(Written at Covenant Presbyterian Church,
Nashville, TN)

Restoration

Lord, You accept us as we are
With all our warts and knobbiness.
You're looking for a yielded heart
And a soul willing to say yes.

After we yield, change will begin
With You working within our heart.
All change will happen at your pace
As You start to set us apart.

Patience is what we need to have
As we wait upon God above.
This is His project to complete
And He does it with such great love.

(Written while flying from Tucson, AZ to Atlanta,
GA on the way to Nashville, TN)

Life

Life is full of blessings and love.
They're ours to seek and find and take.
If we will set our heart aright
Then these things a good life will make.

God is waiting for you to act,
To accept Him and take His word.
He will patiently wait for you
Until from your heart He has heard,

He'll guide you ev'ry step you take.
Each time He will help you get through.
Life will not always be easy,
With God you will ever ensue.

(Written while flying from Tucson, AZ to Atlanta,
GA on the way to Nashville, TN)

Involvement

You are a member of God's flock,
It's Christ that you do represent.
It is God's will that must be done
To honor Christ whom God has sent.

What is your role within the flock?
What is the way that you do serve?
You are saved by the grace of God,
Your service then He does deserve.

The Christian's call's to be involved,
To participate in the work.
Involvement makes the Christian grow,
Our duty then we must not shirk.

(Written while sitting in the sanctuary of Covenant
Presbyterian Church, Nashville, TN)

Glorify God

Lord, You alone can search my heart.
In depth You probe with keen insight
Discerning all my inward thoughts,
Bringing my blackness to the light.

Lord God reveal my grievous ways
Then fully purge, forgive my sin.
Put me in right relationship
Then blot out all of earth's loud din.

In Your way that's everlasting
Lead me on Your path that is true
That ev'ry aspect of my life
Will forever glorify You.

(Psalm 139:24)
(Written while sitting in the sanctuary of Covenant
Presbyterian Church, Nashville, TN)

God's Instrument

Do your eyes sparkle because of God's
    love?
Does God's love put a smile on your face?
Are your cheeks rosy from God's tender
    touch?
Does your radiance reflect God's grace?

Are your ears open to receive God's Word,
To gently hear your neighbor's heart plea?
Does your mouth speak only that which is
    kind,
Sharing God's love ever so gently?

Are your hands open for welcoming all,
To pray for those who have a deep need?
Are your arms wide ready to give a hug
And to uplift those who're wearied?

Is your mouth kept closed tight so you can
    hear
Grieving sighs of one who needs to share,
To be the gentle and strong quiet one,
Be the presence that shows you do care?

Is your shoulder always available
To a friend who has a broken heart,
To bring loving comfort and assurance
That from them God will never depart?

Are both your feet shod and ready to go,
To go any place that God does call,
To be His feet and to be His strong hands
To be His servant to one and all?

Wholly Thine

Lord teach us to hallow Your name.
Show us how to treasure Your grace.
Help us walk worthy of Your call.
Show us how Your love to embrace.

Lord we know all the correct words
And we speak them with such great ease.
It's our actions we need to hone
So that to You our lives would please.

Lord we want to be wholly Thine
In each spoken word and each deed.
Help us grow in knowing Your Word
That we can ever plant Your seed.

Gracious Love

O Lord, You are the creator of all,
You are the author and breather of life.
For life You are the one who does maintain.
For each of us You have a special call.

Our life belongs to You and You alone.
All of our service is offered to You.
Our life should be a reflection of You.
Every facet of our life You hone.

Our stubbornness and our wandering heart
Have put us on a path away from You.
Your gracious heart and Your long-suffering
Await our return from our wayward start.

Although we have wandered so far from
    You,
You gently welcome us into Your arms.
Your patient love and Your kind forgiveness
Draw us to have You in all that we do.

(Written while sitting in the sanctuary of Covenant
Presbyterian church, Nashville, TN)

The Call

Christ called Lazarus to come forth
To rise from death, walk from the cave.[1]
Christ calls the weary and laden
To come to Him and He will save.[2]

God has called each of us by name[3]
A holy calling He did make.[4]
He called in sanctification,[5]
A sacred calling for His sake.

Wisely consider your calling,[6]
Be certain of His calling you.[7]
For you were called in the one hope[8]
That He may count you worthy too.[9]

God's calling's irrevocable.[10]
Walk to be worthy of the call.[11]
Partakers of a call from heav'n[12]
Press toward the goal, stand up tall.[13]

(Written while visiting Linda and Darryl
Amy in Greenfield, IN)

---

1. John 11:43
2. Matthew 11:28
3. Isaiah 43:1
4. 2 Timothy 1:9
5. 1 Thessalonians 4:7
6. 1 Corinthians 1:26
7. 2 Peter 1:10
8. Ephesians 4:4
9. 2 Thessalonians 1:11
10. Romans 11:29
11. Ephesians 4:1
12. Hebrews 3:1
13. Philippians 3:14

Follow Christ

What does it take to follow Christ –
Deny self and have all as loss,
Which is quite a difficult task,
And then one must take up the cross.

Our identity must be lost,
No longer are we in control.
Our life is pointed to the Christ,
For He's the savior of our soul.

No longer are we the master.
Now we're the trusted loyal slave,
Loyal to our savior and Lord.
It's only Him our life can save.

Nothing this earthly life offers
Can fulfill our every need.
Only by taking up the cross
Can our inner soul truly feed.

(Written at the Ash Wednesday service at
Covenant Presbyterian Church, Nashville, TN)

God Is Calling

God is calling, calling for you,
Seeking you wherever you are,
Searching for you with His great love,
Whether you're near or gone afar.

God's desire is to be your friend
And then to be your loving Lord.
He wants to give you life anew,
Laving blessings you can't afford.

Stitch your heart to those heaven bound.
Let your heart sing a brand new song.
Experience life all anew
As part of Christ's amazing throng.

(Written while visiting Marilyn and Tom Dumm in
Naples, FL)

God of Cleansing

Gracious God in heaven above,
The source of life, amazing love,
How awesome is Your majesty
Displayed in ev'rything I see.

Though such a sinful man am I,
Whose sinful ways are piled high,
Yet still my blackened soul You seek
E'en through the stench my sins do reek.

Pursuing and relentless God,
You are there where ever I trod.
No matter where I try to hide
You're always there right at my side.

Oh God of grace and of mercy,
From Satan's bonds please set me free.
Wash my soul of each sinful blot
So that in hell my soul won't rot.

Remove me from this sinful plight
And garb me in a robe of white.
Make me to be clean, wholly Thine,
That ever with Thee I may dine.

(Written while visiting Marilyn and Tom Dumm in
Naples, FL)

Costly Grace

Extravagant grace bought by Christ,
At the cost of His earthly life.
He bore our sin upon the cross
To redeem us from earthly strife.

In turn what is the price we pay,
Or do we deem it just our right?
Since Christ did pay the heavy price
Are we covered without a fight?

Grace demands we pick up our cross
And pursue true discipleship.
Grace demands we embrace the Christ,
So through our fingers He won't slip.

Grace demands contrition for sin,
So deliverance can be made.
The sinner will be justified
Based on the price that he has paid.

Only God can provide us grace,
And for that we must pay the cost.
Our whole life is the total price,
If we don't pay, then we are lost.

Walking Life's Path

As with your life you sullenly brood,
Remember life's not about your mood.
It's about how you decide to live
And the legacy you want to give.

Let curiosity be your guide
As leisurely down life's path you stride.
Rejoice and give honor and applaud
Commending all on the path you trod.

Live your life in the current moment
With lots of squiggles of enjoyment.
Have laughter be a part of your talk
As joyful with the Christ you do walk.

Coping

Lord, we are wounded and are scarred,
Beaten down by this earthly life.
We struggle against many taunts
And labor on with all the strife.

We seek for mercy, plead for help,
We seek relief and just get sneers.
We persevere and carry through
Finding comfort in all our tears.

We thank you God for all your grace.
You are our strong sufficient hope.
We do praise You through all our days.
It's by Your strength that we can cope.

Silence

Lord, how wonderful is this place.
Here Your Holy spirit does grace.
Here our life's troubles we can face.
Here life takes on a slower pace.

The silence is a comfort too.
It's special quiet time with You.
Here such great peace You do imbue,
And here Your blessings are not few.

Here the restless spirit is calm.
Here we find Your Gilead balm.
It's here that life does not have qualm,
And joys of life burst forth in psalm.

Amazing silence you employ.
For with this our fears You destroy
And life's foibles do not annoy.
In Your presence, life is a joy.

(Written while sitting alone in the sanctuary of
Covenant Presbyterian Church, Nashville, TN)

Protection

God is our fortress and our shield.
He's there to supply all our need.
His arms enfold us, draw us close
And by His hand, us He does feed.

When tumults assault on our way,
When trials overwhelm our heart,
God is there standing strong and firm,
And from us He will ne'er depart.

Come and see the works of our God
Who brings us peace beyond compare.
Come experience gracious love
That God does abundantly share.

Come and exalt the Lord of all
And submit to His gentle prod.
Reverence Him in all you do;
Be still and know that He is God.

(Inspired by Psalm 46)

Pleasing God

What is it that would please the Lord?
Is it sacrifices we bring?
Is it our reading of the Word?
Is it the hymns and songs we sing?

Is it the words that we do speak?
Is it the sacraments we share?
Is it attendance at the church?
Is it the countenance we wear?

None of these will justify us!
In all the ways that we do trod,
We're to do justice, love mercy,
And to walk humbly with our God.

(Micah 6:8)

Good Morning, Lord

Good morning, Lord, it's another day.
Please help me to do all things Your way.
I do not know what Your plan might be.
I pray that whate'er, You can use me.

As I greet others, may they just see
The presence of Christ instead of me.
May each word I speak carry Your love
And warm hearer's heart by Your sweet
   Dove.

May actions be a mirror to all,
Reflecting Christ, so on Him they'll call.
I'm available, use me O Lord
As a living display of Your Word.

(Written while at Lake Junaluska, North Carolina)

Love Shows Through

The palm fronds were preserved with care
And then with fire were turned to ash.
That common residue was blessed,
And changed to sacred in a flash.

A symbolic continuing
Of God's love that the Christ did live,
E'en through crucifixion and death,
That love of God the Christ does give.

Through God's love true life we do gain
And that love should give us a glow,
So that as others perceive us
God's love, through us, will ever show.

(Written at Grace Place Church)

Lenten Growth

Forty days in the wilderness
Is where temptations Christ did face.
Christ persevered, won the challenge,
With His Father's mercy and grace.

Lent is our time of sacrifice
To revere what Christ did endure.
With citations from God's Own Word
We, like Christ, have temptation's cure.

As we experience the Lent
May we closer to the Christ grow.
Through each of our word and act
May the love of Christ ever show.

(Written at the Donelson-Hermitage YMCA)

Change

Parades, parties, under way,
And they'll persist throughout the day.
On they'll go throughout the night,
They'll end before the dawning light.

Rid the deleterious store
So the bad fat stuff is no more.
Clear the body and clean the heart
For on the morrow Lent does start.

As Lenten time begins it phase
Will you endure for forty days?
As o'er your life your deeds are cast
In your life, what changed that will last?

(Written at the Donelson-Hermitage YMCA)

Verify

We're God's sheep, but do we follow?
Do we harken unto His voice?
Do we submit unto His lead
Or do we go with our own choice?

What is the voice we claim to hear?
Is it truly the voice of God?
Or is it an imagined word
That only comes when we do nod?

Be sure you verify the source
Of what you let into your ear.
God's message that comes through His
voice
Will be the same as His Word so dear.

(Written at the Donelson-Hermitage YMCA)

The Sheep

I am a sheep, just wan'dring 'round.
If in the pasture's where I'm found,
Then I'm content, you'll not confound,
'Cause with the Lord I'm homeward bound.

My shepherd's voice I thus do heed.
He leads to pastures where I feed.
He provides for all of my need.
His supply far exceeds my greed.

If I follow the shepherd's way
He'll keep me safe throughout each day.
Within his fold I safely stay.
He protects me so I won't stray.

(Written at the Donelson-Hermitage YMCA)

Ashes

From the ashes us God did make.
His Spirit infused us with breath.
With us God sought companionship,
If we'd obey we'd not face death.

Obedience brought endless joy,
Do God's will and do it His way.
Deviate from that, pay the price,
To ashes then we would decay.

The Lenten ashes do remind
That we were drawn by God's own hand.
Our mortality's limited,
Eternity with God is grand.

(Written at Grace Place Church)

Lent

Just how do you respond to Lent?
Is it a drudge or is it joy?
Is it a time to hibernate
Or time to be in God's employ?

Our attitude will set the pace
Of how, in Lent, we will respond.
Will it be duty diligence
Or with God make a stronger bond?

Lent's a time to review our life
So closer to God we can grow.
A time to find new service paths
Wherein through us God's love will show.

(Written at Grace Place Church)

Spring Time

Love blooms eternal in spring time,
A message of hope to declare.
Resurrection time's drawing nigh
As new life blossoms ev'rywhere.

A recurring sign does appear
Troubling our sinuses with flair.
It interrupts what ere we do
As the pollens do fill the air.

With all the newness of spring time
Our spirit is enlivened too.
Joviality fills the air,
For each day let the Son shine through.

(Written at Grace Place Church)

Rest

As you carry out your life's plan
And persevere on your life's quest
How do you gauge progress you make?
Where in your plan do you find rest?

Is rest important to your way
Or just a task that you eschew?
Is rest something you enjoy
Or just a blight that you must do?

Rest is a need to balance life
So a full life you can pursue.
Lord help me to really seek rest,
True rest that's only found in You.

(Written at the Donelson-Hermitage YMCA)

Memories

As memories flow through our mind
Be sure that there we do not dwell.
Live through this day, it's all we have,
For Christ we need to live it well.

Each day new memories we do build,
Mem'ries that build throughout the year.
The best of mem'ries include Christ
And how the Christ did hold us near.

Mem'ries with Christ we oft should share,
They can encourage us each day.
The more we fill our life with Christ,
From Him, well done we'll hear Him say.

(Written at the Donelson-Hermitage YMCA)

Content

Is Jesus your sufficiency
Or is more ever your lament?
Is Jesus your Jehovah Jireh,
In His supply are you content?[1]

Is Christ enough in all your ways
Including time with the sages?
Does Christ's supply give you comfort
To be content with your wages?[2]

Does Christ help you to be content
In the circumstances you face?[3]
Are you content with what you have[4]
And give Jesus thanks for His grace?

---

1. 1 Timothy 6:8
2. Luke 3:14
3. Philippians 4:11
4. Hebrews 13:5

God's Ways

Each day does seem to have its fill
Of very many things to do.
Special days make it more complex,
And maybe we can't follow through.

Our special days have no affect
On what, for us, the Lord has planned.
Our scheming ways centered on self
Are trivial in God's scheme so grand.

Our constant following God's ways
Is where life's progress will be made.
Thus, persevere along God's path,
You'll find His blessings will not fade.

(St. Patrick's Day)
(Written at the Donelson-Hermitage YMCA)

Desire

Christ ever faced situations
And handled each with such calm grace.
He did not react, just respond
And with each, teaching He did lace.

A great example for our life
As oft we face situations.
Pause, exhale, then take a deep breath,
Be laved with God's inspirations.

Peace, tranquility are great traits
To calm, assuage our ev'ry ire.
Peace that passeth understanding
Should ever be our heart's desire.

(Written at the Donelson-Hermitage YMCA)

Thanks

Our priority's giving thanks,
For God's deserving of our thanks,
Adoration and praise and thanks.
E'en for our life we should give thanks.

Christ should be adorned with our thanks,
For His love we give Him thanks.
For each breath we take, give God thanks,
For forgiveness we give God thanks.

We give God praise by giving thanks,
We receive grace when we give thanks.
We learn to love through giving thanks,
We are blessed when we give God thanks.

Live for Christ

Have you surrendered all to Christ,
Put Him on the throne of your heart,
Yielded to Him control of your life,
Let Him give your life a new start?

Has Christ convicted you of sin?
Have you repented, cleansed your soul?
Have you confessed your sinful ways?
Have you turned life to His control?

Have you found contentment in Christ?
Have you found peace that God does give?
Have you found joy that has no bound?
For Christ, are you ready to live?

Our God

O Lord, You are an awesome God,
You are beyond our fathoming.
Your grace is so magnanimous,
Your presence ever peace does bring.

You do provide beyond our need,
You give us strength to carry on.
Perseverance for us You bless,
From You, abundant life we've won.

Your amazing love has no end,
Forgiveness of sin You do give.
You answer ev'ry prayer we raise,
Only through You true life we live.

(Written at the Donelson-Hermitage YMCA)

Duties

Old man time has just passed the torch,
The new young babe is now in charge.
Transfer celebrations are done
And the babe's duties are quite large.

For many 'tis another day,
Their one change is the year number.
For some, it's tears that they embrace
For ones in eternal slumber.

One thing did not change, God still reigns,
Pouring blessings on all His kin.
He'll continue to work with us,
Still forgiving us of our sin.

(Written at the Donelson-Hermitage YMCA)

Clan

We set our mind to do what's right,
We'll get it done 'cause we are tough.
We will pursue and persevere,
Good intentions are not enough.

Our actions are the deeds that count,
Those actions will produce results.
After the fact, the words are fine,
Prior words may just be insults.

The same holds true e'en for our faith.
Following God and His best plan
Will yield results beyond our thought
And make us part of God's great clan.

(Written at the Donelson-Hermitage YMCA)

Essence of Love

It's bitter cold, no need to pout,
Use it as a reason to shout.
Living life's what it's all about,
We'll get through the cold 'cause we're
  stout.

This cold is part of God's array,
E'en through this, blessings He'll display.
Let Christ lead you throughout this day,
Be strong in Him, follow His way.

Wear the Christ as a well-fit glove,
Keeping your eyes on Him above,
For Christ is God's heavenly Dove,
And Christ is the essence of love.

(Written at the Donelson-Hermitage YMCA)

I Love You So

Jesus, to You I offer thanks.
On me, Your Spirit You bestow.
How do I share just how I feel?
I love You so, I love You so.

Your kindness is beyond compare.
From You, blessings do ever flow.
My heart You ever strangely warm.
I love You so, I love You so.

My soul daily You do nourish.
Grace upon grace You ever show.
My soul ever does yearn for You.
I love You so, I love You so.

The Love Of God

God loves us though we are sinners,[1]
God's love is of a special kind.
God's love is something you can't buy,
God's love, the best jewel to find.

God's love is something you can't earn.
God's love is well beyond our mind.
God's love is one thing we can't lose.
God's love our heart and soul does bind.

We're God's creation, us He does love.
With God's love we're well entwined.
God's love sustains us through each day.
For God's great love our hearts have pined.

---

1. Romans 5:8

Forevermore

My sinful self I do abhor,
It's only Christ that I adore,
He'll get me safely to the shore,
To live with Him forevermore.

What wondrous blessings are in store
As in the Christ my life does soar.
He fills my life, e'en to the core,
Then live with Him forevermore.

As all my hair does turn to hoar
And gracious times have been my lore
His sweet Spirit on me does pour.
I'll be with Him forevermore.

Love

Love's manifest in many ways,
In use and definition.
For some it is a life-long guide,
For others, there's much transition.

We live to love or love to live,
We love our family and friends.
We love all that we encounter,
We use love for prurient ends.

The best example of true love
Has no trappings and has no fuss.
Amazing love that's full of grace,
Though we're sinners, Christ died for us.

(Written at Grace Place Church)

Christ In Me

My heart and soul do long for Thee
O Savior of humanity.
Though a sinner, to Thee I plead
For cleansing and to fill my need.

Your gracious love I cannot spurn,
I have no other place to turn.
Cover me over with Your veil,
Protect me from those who assail.

Christ, take this wretched soul of mine,
Restore me in Your love divine.
Use my life that others see
It is the Christ who lives in me.

(Written at Grace Place Church)

Christ's Love

He loves me or he loves me not,
The daisy game that children play.
It may suffice a childish whim,
'Tis not a part of Jesus' way.

Jesus' love is of agape,
Not earned and no way you can buy.
Self-surrender is all it takes
To be the apple of Christ's eye.

In Christ's love there's room for one more,
Christ is willing to bring you in.
The one thing you must seek to do
Is ask forgiveness of your sin.

Effort

Veni, the start of another day.
They came for work, or was it play.
They persevered throughout the task,
Stress, elation they did not mask.

Vedi, eyes open to what was ahead.
'Twas not their ego that they fed.
Muscles responded, not a tease,
And there was progress that did please.

Vici, then the task was complete,
They were not dragging on their feet.
A broad smile appeared on each face,
The morning effort God did grace.

(Written at the Donelson-Hermitage YMCA)
(Veni, Vedi, Vici: I came, I saw, I conquered)

The Lord God

The rain has come, yet we'll not melt,
As all those drops on us do pelt.
We'll persevere and will succeed
Because the Lord is all we need.

The rain may make things more a mess
While through it all God still does bless.
God's blessings flow much like the rain,
Each brings its joy, reduces pain.

Renewal keeps us moving on
From early morn, e'en before dawn.
Yield to the Christ, follow His way
And He'll provide a wondrous day.

(Written at the Donelson-Hermitage YMCA)

Provisions From God

We set our plans for the next week,
But God's guidance did we seek?
God's will for our life will be done,
No matter the tales we have spun.

Without God's help we'll reap a mess,
With God involved, us He will bless.
Without God we'll stumble along,
In God's arms is where we belong.

God is our sure strong safety net.
In Him there is no need to fret.
God will use us in His employ
And He will provide us much joy.

(Written at the Donelson-Hermitage YMCA)

That Step

With scale-clogged eyes all things were
   blurred,
Like slogging through a bog of curd.
No sound, not e'en a chirping bird
And then I heard God's gracious Word.

As to that Word I did draw near
I noticed that the way did clear.
Then with purpose and without fear,
A tender voice I then did hear.

With clear open eyes I did see
A glor'us vista before me.
That sweet voice called to set me free,
I took that step and followed Thee.

(Written at Grace Place Church)

Jesus' Love Covers All

Jesus, You're my gracious savior,
You called while I was deep in sin.
You offered me abundant life,
You said with You this fight I'll win.

In midst of my depravity
You gently spoke unto my heart.
Your encouragement, an allure
That from sin-life I could depart.

Oh, woe is me, my heart did plead,
Release me from this dreaded pall.
I took Your hand and then stepped forth
And found Your love does cover all.

(Written at Grace Place Church)

God-View

God's Word is a guide for our life,
Showing us how to live in love,
And how forgiveness we can give,
It's all been sent from God above.

Getting it in our mind is hard,
The next step is the hardest part,
And a great challenge for our life,
Getting it from our mind to our heart.

Once our heart is fully involved
There's no limit what God can do.
Yielding to Him's a wondrous task
Lets us see life with a God-view.

(Written at Grace Place Church)

Remember

Gently the morning rain does fall
Cleansing the air, renewing all.
Those raindrops do a soft-shoe dance
As on hard surfaces they prance.

A cue from the drops we should take
As through our life each step we make.
Gently refreshing words to use,
As Christ in our life does infuse.

A steady pace without a rush
Will then our anxious heart to hush.
Remember Christ, His blood did shed,
And then He rose up from the dead.

(Written at the Donelson-Hermitage YMCA)

The Most

Christ birthed this day for us to live,
And His way to us He did give.
His blessings on us He does pour,
And He'll do that forevermore.

Christ gave us eyes that we would see
His manifestations in me.
Not that I would ever be praised,
But only Christ's name would be raised.

As God's plan for us we pursue
May His love for us e'er shine through.
It's only in Christ that we do boast
Because Christ alone is the most.

(Written at the Donelson-Hermitage YMCA)

Roller Coaster

Weather's playing its funny games,
The roller coaster temps are bold.
They make the swing from day to day.
Do we prepare for hot or cold?

Do we have roller coaster faith?
We're doing fine 'till there is pain.
Things go well then things go awry.
Do we then lose all we did gain?

Father, Son and Holy Spirit
Are consistent in all they do.
Forsake the roller coaster ways,
God will help you to follow through.

(Written at the Donelson-Hermitage YMCA)

Fame

I yield my heart to Thee, O Lord,
That's where I want Your throne to be.
In my life I want You to reign
That all I do will honor Thee.

Open my eyes that I would see
Just what it is that others need.
Open my ears that I would hear
That plaintiff cry as neighbors plead.

Open my arms that I would act
To serve others, all in your name.
Make my presence to fade away
So that the Christ receives the fame.

(Written at Grace Place Church)

God's Love

Nothing can compare with God's love,
It's attributes are unsurpassed.
It can be seen everywhere,
It's reaches are so very vast.

God's love we can not comprehend
Though we do experience it.
Our language limits what we say,
Our descriptive thoughts do not fit.

God's love does not have bounds,
From God's love we can never hide.
God's love completely engulfs us,
God's love will never leave our side.

(Written at Grace Place Church)

Abundant Love

It's a day to celebrate love
And the amenities in store.
We show our love in many ways,
With candy, cards, some hugs and more.

From younger days through adult phase
Our love expressions ever flow.
Not limited to special times,
God's gracious love does ever show.

As Valentine love we express,
And with the multitude we share,
Remember Christ's abundant love
Is poured on us everywhere.

(Written at the Donelson-Hermitage YMCA)

The Rose

A red rose, a Valentine treat,
Another expression of love.
A tender gesture that endures
As its aroma wafts above.

There is a rose that we recall,
Its sweet aroma pleases God.
It reminds us to live in love,
A love to share where e'er we trod.

The Rose of Sharon e'er does glow
And showers us abundantly.
It is the love that never fails
Through our life and eternity.

(Written at the Donelson-Hermitage YMCA)

Ev'ry Moment

Valentine's Day, the day of love,
Yet God is love every day.
Days and seasons are at our whim,
God and His love always hold sway.

This day special treats we share,
With these our love we do express.
God's love's special all the time,
And ever He knows our address.

Celebrate love with each other
And include God in that display.
Remember God's love's always there
For ev'ry moment of each day.

(Written at the Donelson-Hermitage YMCA)

Leaning On Christ

Eagerly seek for Christ to help,
Vict'ry's ever in Christ's control.
Our life is in His faithful hands,
Leading us to His perfect role.

Each time we seek some help from Christ
Valued response we will receive.
Often we'll get only silence.
Learn that silence helps us believe.

Earnestly studying God's Word,
Validating your perspective
Of how we're to live in God's love,
Leaves no doubt of God's directive.

God Does Reign

We're heading out on our own way,
Self-leading oft results in pain.
If we would pause and think it through,
We would realize that God does reign.

Reviewing life, its twists and turns,
Pursuing on through sun and rain,
We'd quickly find instances where
It wasn't self, 'twas God did reign.

When on we go with God in lead
There's always much that we do gain.
As with the Lord we persevere,
Life's always best when God does reign.

(Written at the Donelson-Hermitage YMCA)

Special Treasure

My weary soul cries out to God,
My sinful self does yearn for Thee.
Daily I struggle through my pain.
In Christ's arms is where I should be.

The Christ does hear my moaning cry,
My sin Christ ever does forgive.
Christ strengthens me e'en through my pain,
Nestled in Christ's arms I can live.

The love of Christ is broad and deep
And that love is beyond measure.
Christ inundates us with His love
And that love's a special treasure.

(Written at the Donelson-Hermitage YMCA)

The Lead

Who do you follow as your lead?
Who gives you guidance for the way?
Who provides guard rails for your life
So from the path you will not stray?

If you've set self as your life's lead
Remember you are still finite,
And when you exhaust all of self,
You still will be amid the plight.

There's only one you can follow
Whose supply does have no limit.
That one is Christ, God's only Son
And into His way you can fit.

(Written at the Donelson-Hermitage YMCA)

Serve

God will supply all of your need,
Of His supply there is no end.
All we have to do is just ask,
Supply comes from our faithful Friend.

Do we express our gratitude
And give thanks for all God does do?
Do we take time through all our rush
To thank God, who carries us through?

Thankful should be our way of life,
Thanks from us the Lord does deserve.
Share appreciation with Him
Because Him alone we should serve.

(Written at the Donelson-Hermitage YMCA)

Amazing Love

God give to us amazing love
That has no limit and no end.
So undeserving we'll still be,
For us Christ died, our hearts to mend.

Broken and sinful is our state,
Christ gave His life, us to redeem.
Christ opened the flood gates of love
That shines with radiant beam.

Christ loves us, of that there's no doubt.
Though sinners, us Christ does not spurn.
Christ's amazing love e'er does flow
And what do we do in return?

(Written at Grace Place Church)

Shepherd

We are like sheep, need a leader,
A strong guide that won't let us stray.
One who knows of the green pastures
And leads us there from day to day.

Christ's our shepherd, provides our need,
Streams of living water He'll show.
In green pastures He lets us graze
And on us His love does bestow.

Daily He feeds us from His Word,
Nourishing our heart and our soul,
To make us sleek and trim and fit
That ever Him we would extol.

(Written at Grace Place Church)

I Am God

Our life is full of hustle and rush,
Hurry's the mantra of the day.
Patience is an anathema
And there's no place for it to play.

In our frenetic head-long dash,
Instant success we do pursue.
When we reach the end of the day,
Our mind is tied on what to do.

We need to pause, and really stop
And slow the pace of how we trod.
Apply God's Word to all of life,
Be still and know that I am God.[1]

(Written at Grace Place Church)

---

1. Psalm 46:10

Gratitude

Lord, fill our heart with gratitude
Then let us pour that upon You.
You always do so much for us
And all Your ways are ever true.

We accept, but do we give thanks?
You mete so much abundant grace
Regardless of how we do act,
Do words of thanks escape our face?

Give thanks, oft we should be doing.
Every moment we should thank You
For all Your love and Your blessings
And for us, wondrous things You do.

(Written at Grace Place Church)

True Life

We make the choice of where we live.
That's where our efforts we do give.
We make our own assenting nod
To live quite near or far from God.

Takes more than desire for the task
If one's to live within God's bask.
Many obstacles block our way,
Sin is well schooled in this foray.

Intention must be our first guide
And we must resist all our pride.
We must act within God's own plan
And all detours we need to ban.

The life of grace is like a stool
And its three legs become our tool.
Study, action must be our prayer
True piety must be our share.

For us to share true love indeed,
Living in Christ is what we need.
If we do choose that price to pay,
God will sustain us ev'ry day.

Living Christ's Love

Love is from God and it's for us,
Christ showed that love upon the cross.
Though sinners, Christ died for us.[1]
Christ's sacrifice removed our dross.

Christ lived this life displaying love,
A new commandment Christ did give,
That we should love one another,[2]
For that's the way we should live.

God's love for us should move us on,
Our hallmark of life together.
Since God loves us so very much
We ought to love one another.[3]

---

1. Romans 5:8
2. John 13:34
3. 1 John 4:11

My Friend

Jesus, my very special friend,
His love for me does never end.
His graciousness He does extend,
Against Satan He does defend.

Our wounded heart the Christ does mend,
To us His Spirit He did send.
My ways to Him I freely bend
And to my needs He does attend.

Along His ways I freely wend,
With Him I take time to spend.
With His last breath the veil did rend,
Ever to Him my ears I lend.

(Written at the Donelson-Hermitage YMCA)

Walking With Christ

Each day it starts when you awake,
Before your feet do hit the floor,
Your daily walk with Jesus Christ,
The One who gives blessings galore.

Christ will rejuvenate your heart,
Be sure each day to Him you yield.
Follow the plan He has for you
And He will be your faithful shield.

Be sure a broad smile you do wear
And through you, Christ's love's on display.
Make effort others to affirm
And that oft you take time to pray.

(Written at the Donelson-Hermitage YMCA)

Carries

I have my plan set for this day,
'Tis a long list of things to do.
If Christ was not the center piece,
Then my great plan cannot be true.

We are tasked to follow Christ's way
If His disciples we're to be.
These are the words Christ did offer,
Leave all behind, come follow Me.

Christ's yoke's easy, His burden, light
For each step, He's right there with you.
Though we stumble and take a fall,
Christ picks us up, carries us through.

(Written at the Donelson-Hermitage YMCA)

The Best Gift

What is the best gift we can give
As through this earthly life we live?
It's not some trinket off the shelf,
The best gift to give is our self.

Christ wants each moment of our life
To be filled with much joy, not strife.
Christ leads us on His perfect way
Following Him every day.

Christ loves us, for us He does care
And in our life He wants to share.
He wants us to shine ev'rywhere.
Thus, what kind of fruit do you bear?

(Written at the Donelson-Hermitage YMCA)

Pure

'Tis in Christ we can truly live.
Christ's abundance on us does pour.
Christ loves us with an endless love.
Blessings He always has in store.

Our countenance is based on Christ.
Our joy's a decision of the heart.
Our attitude directs our act.
Centered on Christ is life's best start.

Discipleship does take effort,
Perseverance you must endure.
Christ always gives what's best for you,
All that He gives is ever pure.

(Written at the Donelson-Hermitage YMCA)

God And Man

In the garden, God walked with man
And rich fellowship they did share.
God's deep desire was for those times
Because He's a God who does care.

Then the fellowship was broken,
Man had stepped away from God's side.
Man broke that special bond of love
And then from God, the man did hide.

Disappointment confronted God,
Fellowship's desire in His heart.
Man was the cause of that great rift,
From the garden man must depart.

God's fellowship desire still burned
And remained unassailable.
God seeks that fellowship with man.
Are you one that's available?

Bear

The Lion bears all of our guilt,
The Lion is our redeemer.
Even bears bow to the Lion,
For the Lion is our creator.

We're admonished to share burdens,
And yet our load we are to bear.
Our sharing is an act of love
And demonstrates how much we care.

All of the creatures God did make
And a purpose for each is there.
Cherish ev'rything God has made,
Including a lonely and wild bear.

(Written at a Writers Workshop)

Silence

Silence, a challenge to our way,
Solace we can appropriate.
Serenity will come along,
The peace we will appreciate.

Christ would slip away from the crowd,
Silence would join Him on the way.
Solace and comfort He would gain
As to His Father He did pray.

Silence can bring us close to God
As life's frenzy we set aside.
Christ's peace settles our heart and soul
As in the Christ we do abide.

(Written at Grace Place Church)

God's Faithfulness

God's faithfulness is very strong
And has endured for many years.
He's walked us through gains and sorrows
And in His bottle put our tears.

With those in the past, He was there,
Now for our raucous life He tends.
Next day's solemnity He'll grace,
Yes, His faithfulness has no ends.

Take a pause, give thanks to the Lord,
In His faithfulness we can bask.
He provides for all of our needs
And guides us through each daily task.

(Written at Grace Place Church)

Wait

Walking was the transportation,
No other way was on the scene.
Running an option rarely used
Slow and easy was what was seen.

The pace of life has greatly changed,
Not by God's doing, but by man.
Hie, rush and haste our way of life,
So try and catch me if you can.

Our rushing pace consumes our time,
Ever fearing we will be late,
While on the side-lines of our life
The Lord does patiently await.

(Written at the Donelson-Hermitage YMCA)

Pray

Always is the right time to pray,
Whether it's night or even day.
It could be at work or at play,
It helps to keep Satan at bay.

If in God's will you want to stay,
Prayer is the key to keep that way,
To get you out of miry clay,
And to bask in the Son's bright ray.

Shed God's light through earth's dark
    display,
And to settle every fray,
Put on Christ's brightening array.
It all will happen if you pray.

(Written at the Donelson-Hermitage YMCA)

Witness

As we are approaching God's house,
Take a brief moment on the way
Collect our worries, aches, concerns,
Hang them on the trees that do sway.

Enter in God's house unburdened,
With hearts and souls awash in joy,
Yielded to the Spirit's leading,
Our life ready for God's employ.

Invest us in worship of You,
Let all our being You extol.
Quicken our being, send us forth
To witness under Your control.

(Written at Grace Place Church)

Claim

We make our claim on this and that,
With vigor we protect our plot.
The Lord has staked His claim on us,
As for our soul in love He fought.

He digs into our sacred vein
Where special jewels He does find.
God's lapidary genius shows,
He knows our mother lode and kind.

Each life is a rich treasure trove
Of sparkling jewels for the Lord.
Let that mine shaft be a river
To brighten displays of God's Word.

(Written at Grace Place Church)

Share

If you're burdened, laden with care
And a smile is not on your face,
Joy's left you standing at the gate,
Because now you are slow of pace.

God's Spirit is alive in you,
A prisoner of your down mood.
You jailer, set that Spirit free
So God's love can be understood.

Open your heart, spirit and mind
To abundance God has for you.
It's in God's freedom you can live
And share His love in all you do.

(Written at Grace Place Church)

Confession

Confession is good for the soul,
Also good for the heart and mind.
It rejuvenates the spirit,
That is where solace you can find.

Confession's on the path to God,
Without it life would be a mess.
Yet that one step will clear the way
To have the Holy Spirit bless.

Confession's our ally in life,
A stepping stone to God's great grace.
It always strengthens our resolve,
Prepares us the next test to face.

(Written at the Donelson-Hermitage YMCA)

Follow

Do you know where you are going
As you start this day of your life?
Are you prepared for anything,
Or just a toot upon your fife?

God has a plan designed for you
To bring you ever close to Him,
To be your guide and to protect
As with alligators you swim.

Persevere within God's comfort
As in His love you do abide.
Follow His plan with confidence,
For He will be right at your side.

(Written at the Donelson-Hermitage YMCA)

Jehovah Jireh

The day's begun, task list is long,
Yet in Christ is where I belong.
Through it all, He will keep me strong
And in my heart He puts a song.

Through it all, in Him I can see
To be who He wants me to be.
For bountiful life, Christ's the key,
In Christ alone then I am free.

With perseverance I'll get through,
Christ's Spirit, my life He'll imbue.
His love will ever keep me true
So Christ is seen in all I do.

(Written at the Donelson-Hermitage YMCA)

The Cross

The cross, a device to cause death.
A symbol of eternal love,
An invitation to forgive,
Assurance from the heav'nly Dove.

It's the place to confess our sin,
Where eternal life does begin,
Where we escape from the world's din
And where salvation we can win.

It's the start of abundant life
Where we can be filled with God's grace.
It's where hope eternal does shine.
The cross helps us, this life to face.

(Written at the Donelson-Hermitage YMCA)

Thanks

The Lord is doing wondrous things
In our life and with great effect.
His love for us does overflow,
We receive more than we expect.

There is so much that we receive
Moment by moment, day by day.
How often do we take the time
To pause, give thanks as we do pray?

It is the Thanksgiving season,
Yet our life should ever give thanks.
Categorizing use of time,
Thanks should be in the upper ranks.

(Written at Grace Place Church)

Give Thanks

Give thanks that Advent is at hand,
Anticipation's in the air.
Give thanks for expected new birth,
The birth that frees us from despair.

Give thanks that Christ did come to earth
As fully God and fully man.
Give thanks to God for His great grace
And for His great salvation plan.

Give thanks that each of us God loves
And that in Him we can be free.
Give thanks to God for forgiveness
So we are His eternally.

(Written at Grace Place Church)

Christ's Presence

It's early morning, dark the cloud
And some crying the cloud will do.
Like the rain drops, the temp will drop.
Thankfully Christ carries us through.

With the vagaries life does bring,
More the blessings Christ does bestow.
He's ever watchful, fills our need.
In His presence our life will glow.

The outward look may seem so drear,
But inward Christ is always near
To bring us comfort, bring us cheer.
Thus with the Christ we need not fear.

(Written at the Donelson-Hermitage YMCA)

Thanks

Lord, thank You for the gift of life.
Thank You for sending us Your Son.
Thank You for Your salvation plan
And the mighty works You've begun.

Thanks for the privilege of prayer
And for the answers that You give.
Thanks for being our strength and guide.
Thank You through strife, You help us live.

Thanks for blessings and grace You share.
Thanks for Your presence ev'rywhere.
Thanks for strengthening us each day.
Thanks, You are a God who does care.

(Written at the Donelson-Hermitage YMCA)

New Day

The morn is brisk, temps near freezing,
That doesn't mean that God is snoozing.
Our warm bed is quite comforting.
Through all this, God still brings blessing.

We yield, and get up from the bed,
Make sure our body has been fed.
We walk God's Word as He has led,
For forgiveness, to God we've pled.

We step forth to begin the day,
After we took good time to pray
That God would keep Satan at bay
And that from God we'll never stray.

(Written at Grace Place Church)

New Song

God provides our heart a new song,
And with that song the Lord we praise.
As we sing and lift up His name,
We find our spirits He does raise.

A song can soothe our aching heart,
Closer to God that song does bring.
Each step toward God that we do take
Lifts our spirit, makes our soul sing.

Keep eyes and thoughts focused on God.
Be intentional in your ways.
Be diligent and persevere
And Christ will bless each of your days.

(Written at the Donelson-Hermitage YMCA)

Soar

It's the time of year for changes
And the weather has joined the show.
The dark of night grows much longer,
The wind provides a heady blow.

Through all the changes we endure,
And the shenanigans and pranks,
The Lord is constant, does not change.
For that blessing we give Him thanks.

The Lord's blessings are ever new,
Abundantly these He does pour.
With His gracious and tender love
Through each new day we then can soar.

Kyrie Eleison

Lord, I have wandered from Your path
And am deserving of Your wrath.
Immerse me in Your cleansing bath.
Kyrie eleison.

I've read, but not followed Your ways.
'Twas my own trail I tried to blaze.
Now I find myself in a daze.
Kyrie eleison.

I've come to You seeking Your rest.
I've found Your ways to be the best.
You are the ending of my quest.
Kyrie eleison.

(Kyrie eleison – Lord have mercy)

His Plan

We think we have things well in hand
And then we find one more demand.
There is much more than we had planned
And one more task I'll not withstand.

I'll do my best to persevere,
Complaints from me you will not hear.
My path is fixed as God does steer.
With Him I share a happy tear.

God's plan for me is the best way
And with His plan I'll try to stay.
God even gives me time to play,
If daily to Him I do pray.

(Written at the Donelson-Hermitage YMCA)

That Hand

God stretches forth a healing hand.
That hand has scars where nails were thrust.
That hand delivers gracious love
And ever it's a hand that's just.

That hand can calm the raging soul.
That hand can heal each aching part.
That hand brings joy to downcast ones.
That hand can soothe the broken heart.

That hand brings strength to the weary.
That hand brings arms that can enfold.
That hand can guide you on God's path.
That hand and arms give hugs so bold.

Near

The many details of our life
Are the source of most of our strife.
Concentration there is not bliss,
And much of life we thus do miss.

Christ faced the details that we face
And handled each with so much grace.
Frustration oft He did endure
Because us earthlings are not pure.

Unto Christ daily we should grow
So His ways we can better know.
With Christ we can even face fear,
Thus we should always keep Christ near.

(Written at the Donelson-Hermitage YMCA)

Celebrate

The days are just moving along,
With an incessant pace they creep.
Last minute stuff, you may be late.
Take courage, you don't need to weep.

Preparation's secondary,
Importance is in the event.
Expectation is the season
As we're near the end of Advent.

Rest now is an important thing
So you're ready to celebrate.
Give all your being to the Christ,
For His blessings are never late.

(Written at the Donelson-Hermitage YMCA)

Love

The air is cold, the night is long,
Trials besiege on ev'ry day.
We wonder just how we will cope,
Love's journey doesn't come this way.

We bundle up and do our best,
But that is never quite enough.
We struggle, yet we persevere,
With love, life would not be so rough.

On Christmas day, love came to earth,
That love is here for ev'ry one.
Love is a free gift from the Lord.
That love is Christ, God's only Son.

One Task

My to-do list is quite long
And progress on it is quite slow.
I persevere to get things done
And at day's end, little to show.

The day moves on and I'm busy
As I'm about those daily tasks.
And then much to my great surprise,
Gracious Lord, a question does ask.

He asks, why do you struggle so?
With Christ your life's full to the brim.
Each day you've just one task to do
And it is that you follow Him.

Changeless

The holiday is now over,
The packages are all unwrapped.
Fam'ly have returned to their homes
And all our energy is sapped.

Will normalcy ever return
Or has a new norm now been set?
We're thankful for blessings received
And for the new friends we have met.

Through all these days some things don't
   change.
There's the changelessness of God's Word.
God's blessings are still new each day,
And Jesus Christ still reigns as Lord.

(Written at the Donelson-Hermitage YMCA)

Fame

This year is drawing to its close.
Mem'ries of good and bad we share.
We concentrate on happy times
As for a new year we prepare.

The year will start, God's in control.
His center is for us to win.
Our intellectual constructs
End where God's wisdom does begin.

Full abundance of life we seek.
Only through God we'll stake that claim.
Such joy and wonder we'll receive
As God does receive all the fame.

Home

We like to travel, wander off,
To many places we do roam.
Sometimes that travel brings on stress.
We find there is no place like home.

We have been there, explored that place,
Saw many capitals and dome.
We're awed by this, amazed at that.
It's always nice to get back home.

Unique beauty's found in each place.
For each place we could write a tome.
We sensed God wherever we went
And thankful He is in our home.

(Written at the Donelson-Hermitage YMCA)

Ride

Final hours are slipping away,
Then the calendar we will flip.
'Round the world reveries will glow,
Then it's off to the new year's trip.

Changes are what we will face,
Thankful that God will be the same.
His grace and mercy still will flow
And we can still honor His name.

New year will start and then ensue.
Soon we'll settle in the new day.
With God we'll have a glor'ous ride
If we do continue to pray.

(Written at the Donelson-Hermitage YMCA

Approaching God

Such sinful people that we are,
Yet, we dare to approach Your throne.
You do accept our petitions,
We're sinful, still our life You hone.

We live a life that's self-centered,
It has no depth and goes nowhere.
We need You enthroned in our heart,
For abundant life You prepare.

Help us to center life on You,
Guide us on the path we should take.
Reform us into one with You,
All this we ask in Your love's sake.

(Written at the Donelson-Hermitage YMCA)

Besetting Steps

Distractions are our nemesis,
And these beset us ev'ry day.
Always at an importune time,
Whether we are at work or play.

The more Christ is involved in life
The less distractions we will face.
The deeper Christ is in our heart,
The more abundant is His grace.

Plough ahead with our eye on Christ,
And a straighter furrow we'll make,
Not because of our great effort,
But 'cause we follow in Christ's wake.

Display God

I want my life to honor Christ,
Ever reflect His precious name.
I want glory to go to Him,
So that there's nothing I can claim.

My life's an instant in God's scheme,
God's forever and eternal.
My life's a spark, soon fades away,
Through centuries God is faithful.

Lord, for the days that you do grant,
May my life e'er display Your love.
Through all my actions and my words
May others see Your heav'nly Dove.

The Place

Do you have a place just for you,
Where you alone can enter rest?
Where you can get quiet repose
And care, concerns you can divest?

A place just for you and your thoughts,
All inhibitions you release.
All diversions are set aside
As you develop inner peace.

Often you should visit that place
And hie there for your renewal.
Listen intently for God's voice
Yield to Him, He's your crown jewel.

(Written at the Donelson-Hermitage YMCA)

Reprieve

Our sin-centered self is a mess,
Such deviousness we conceive.
Mortal flesh can offer no help,
And great help we need to receive.

An ombudsman we sorely need
To intercede, help us believe,
Be the person who speaks for us,
One that's unbiased, can't deceive.

Our mediator is in heav'n,
Assistance we'd like to achieve.
That mediator's Jesus Christ,
Only Christ can grant a reprieve.

God's Will

David, a man after God's heart,
God, the center of David's life.
God poured blessings upon David,
Guided his ways, kept him from strife.

David's son then became the king,
Concerned how God's people to lead.
God offered him special blessings,
He pled, wisdom is what I need.

God will help us our life to live,
God wants us to tell Him our need,
And like king Solomon's request,
For God's wisdom we each should plead.

False Hope vs Faith

We hope that God will hear our plea.
We hope that we've confessed enough.
We hope our team will win the game.
We hope sin will roll off like slough.

That's not hope, it's wishful thinking.
'Tween faith and false hope, the gap's large.
In false hope there's no sacrifice.
In faith we let God be in charge.

Faith requires that we do confess.
For faith, to Christ our all we give.
Through faith in Christ we stand redeemed.
Faith's reward, in us Christ does live.

Lessons of Lent

We've passed the half-way point of Lent,
Our sacrifice we have maintained.
What preparations have we made
And what new knowledge have we gained?

What new insights have we thus gleaned
Of Christ's doings these forty days?
How has that impacted our heart
And graced our own spiritual ways?

Are Gospel reports all the same?
Do we dig deeper in God's Word?
Do we just skim a surface read
And abide on what we have heard?

Thorn In The Flesh

Paul endured a thorn in the flesh,
He never let it make him grim.
He prayed for relief, God said no,
God's grace was sufficient for him.

Each does face a thorn in the flesh,
Do we face this thing much like Paul?
Do we accept Christ's "no" for us?
Do we even upon God call?

Christ's body riven with a spear[1]
To attest that the Christ was dead.
Do we take our thorn, live in Christ,
Or do we lament, live in dread?

---

1. John 19:33-35

Morning Song

Early morning before the dawn,
A gracious serenade was heard.
Multi-voices with diff'rent parts,
It was the chirping of the birds.

A pleasing melody they sang,
Their anthem they did sweetly raise.
Joyous adoration they sang,
It was their maker they did praise.

We mere humans should take a hint,
Like feathered friends, to start our days
With gracious melody in song
That we, our Redeemer would praise.

(Written at the Donelson-Hermitage YMCA)

Glory

We strive, do well, and be so proud,
Great accomplishment we have made.
As the next project we begin
We note our glory starts to fade.

Is the project the main event
Or's self-glory the driving force?
Glory should be the sweet dessert
And never served as the main course.

Glory is an important trait
To give, but never us to grow.
Put glory in its proper place,
Glory in excelsis Deo.[1]

---

1. Glory in the highest to God

Interruption

Inconvenient, a flashy word,
Interruption is much the same.
The schedule now is out of whack,
You know that you are not to blame.

It's a dilemma that you face,
A choice that you must now resolve.
Stay with the original plan,
Or see how this now will devolve.

Only one point to guide your choice:
Is this just a random event
Or is it a special design
That's meant for you and heaven sent?

Filling Station

Is your tank low, running on fumes?
Are you near empty position?
Divert yourself from other tasks,
Go visit the filling station.

Take no chance about your status,
You don't' need an aberration,
Make this your priority one,
Go visit the filling station.

It's not about the time nor place,
It's all about your intention.
Get refueled and get recharged,
Just go to God's filling station.

Scripture

All Scripture is inspired by God,[1]
Useful for teaching and training.[1]
Remember, it cannot be broken,[2]
For good works, people need training.[3]

Christ used Scripture for His defense[4]
Against Satan, his temptations.[5]
Satan's efforts to entice us
Uses Scripture aberrations.

How immersed in God's Word are you?
Can you use it to bring you through?
To protect you from Satan's darts?
How immersed is God's Word in you?

---

1. 2 Timothy 3:16
2. John 10:35
3. 2 Timothy 3:17

4. Luke 4:4, 8,12
5. Luke 4:3, 7, 9 -11

New Life

Grain must fall into earth and die,[1]
And from it life springs forth anew.[1]
Love this life and you will lose it,[2]
Die to it, new life will come through.[2]

Is it Christ you want to follow[3]
Or will your leader be just you?
Are you ready to take the steps
To allow you to follow through?

In this life now, what needs to die
So in Christ new life can begin?
Each change is hard, but Christ is there.
With Christ, eternal life you can win.

---

1. John 12:24
2. John 12:25
3. John 12:26

Life In Christ

Busy, busy cries out the day,
Tend to my needs, no time to play,
Keep after me, don't go astray,
All other things just keep at bay.

Pay attention, follow my lead.
I am the only thing you need.
It's my ego that you must feed.
Only through me can you succeed.

Christ's way has a different ploy,
It's set so life you can enjoy.
There's no intent to make you coy,
Be effective in His employ.

(Written at the Donelson-Hermitage YMCA)

In Him

My leader is a carpenter.
Each thing He makes is always right.
Each thing He makes is not common
For each is sacred in His sight.

What's the result of our efforts?
Do we commit to follow Him?
Does His light shine through all we do?
Is all our effort just our whim?

Intentionality we need,
Perseverance should be our way.
Good strength from Him we will receive
If in His graciousness we stay.

(Written at the Donelson-Hermitage YMCA)

Peace

Our heart, mind, soul and spirit seek
For conformation of Your love.
We want You to dwell in our heart
To gain Your guidance from above.

Only You can offer us peace,
Peace that passes understanding.
Your hand thus does assuage our fears
And Your presence is commanding.

We yield our mortal self to Thee,
Provide us your wise stratagem,
Ever we'd be Your instrument.
O Lord, Dona nobis pacem.[1]

---

1. Dona nobis pacem - Grant us peace

Effect

We celebrate the birth of Christ,
We celebrate the resurrection.
We celebrate the Eucharist,
Celebrate new birth dedication.

Reflecting on these life events,
What's the impact that each did make?
Was it just a passing fancy
Or permanent change for His sake?

Are we each living examples
Of the message that Christ did bring,
Reflecting the love Christ did live
And effective in witnessing?

Abide

Christ said you must abide in Me
Or fruitfulness you will not see.
Some pruning helps to set you free
For then more fruitfulness you'll be.

We are the branches, Christ the vine.
Each branch, on the stem does dine
And then produces fruit so fine,
Which may be pressed into wine.

Abide in Christ, bask in His love
Which Christ pours out from heav'n above.
That love will fit us like a glove
And make us shine like God's sweet Dove.

Love and Wrath

We do accept that God loves us
As we ambulate on life's path.
Do we accept the other side
Of life and consider God's wrath?

Too often it's half the gospel
We hear and take into our heart.
The other half's about God's wrath,
Which has been deemed the heavy part.

Lord, help us to present Your all
As love and wrath You interplay.
Help us to love in holy fear,
Protect us from Dies Irae.[1]

---

1. Dies Irae - Day of wrath

God's Son

He made the choice to leave His throne,
With mortal flesh He did adorn.
Just one task He had to fulfill,
'Twas His Father's will to be borne.

Then the leaders He did confront
With God's message of how to live,
To honor each without concern
For what they did and also give.

The leaders would have none of it.
Formal credentials, He had none.
The leaders thought He was a rogue,
Did not consider what He'd done.

What's our stance with this man of God?
Do we ask Him our life to hone?
Have we confessed our errant ways?
Thus, kyrie eleison.[1]

---

1. kyrie eleison - Lord have mercy

Precious Name

God is my refuge, my safe cleft,
He is my fortress, ever strong.
He's my safe haven in the storm,
Ever to Him I do belong.

Though I walk Christ's path, I do err,
My errant ways He does forgive.
I do stumble along the way,
He sustains and in Him I live.

Abundant grace on me He laves,
In His strength I can persevere.
Amazing blessings He does pour,
His precious name I do revere.

(Written at the Donelson-Hermitage YMCA)

The Call

The Lord calls each of us to serve,
But do we hear that sacred call?
Are we attentive to God's ways
Or do His words on deaf ears fall?

God's call's part of His plan for us.
If we don't heed, blessings we miss,
And then our life becomes askew,
And wayward ways instead of bliss.

God knows best for what's to be done.
His ways we never should dismiss.
Consider that within God's call
You are called for a time like this.

God Loves You

God loves you, a statement of fact.
God loves you and won't turn His back.
God loves you, wants you as His own.
God loves you, His plan is on track.

God loves you, this you should accept.
God loves you, a gift He does give.
God loves you, something you can't earn.
God loves you and helps you to live.

God loves you, even when you err.
God loves you, your enemies too.
God loves you, an undying love.
God loves you, let that love shine through.

The Cross

The cross, symbol of heinous death.
The cross, symbol of victory.
The cross, symbol of eternal life.
The cross, marker of history.

The cross takes on many a form,
The Latin form's most prevalent.
Accoutrements adorn that form
In liturgy seasons like lent.

The cross is a stark reminder
Of what discipleship does cost.
Inherent gain does far outweigh
The total sum of all that's lost.

Sorrow and Joy

Many things happen in our life
And some of them will make us sad.
Sorrow we will experience,
That doesn't mean that life is bad.

That sorrow may bring tears to eyes.
Those tears may be our salty food.
Our tears God puts in a bottle[1]
Because of love, not 'cause our mood.

Sorrow may catch us for a time.
God's tear collectors He'll deploy.
Then when God's timing is just right
He'll change our sorrow into joy.[2]

---

1. Psalm 56:8 (ESV)
2. John 16:20 (ESV)

Witness

Lord, You've graced us with a new day,
A privilege we can enjoy.
As we engage today's events
May we be in Your full employ.

Your guidance we do ever need.
For us You know just what is best.
Ere keep us close to Your dear heart.
No matter what will be our quest.

May we ever honor Your name.
May we, Your love, ever reflect.
May all our life be a witness
To show it's You we did select.

(Written at the Donelson-Hermitage YMCA)

Tapestry

God takes all our needs and wants,
Along with our deeds and failings.
Mixes in our concerns, errors,
Adds a dash of all our yearnings.
Takes a cup of abilities
And a dash of our shortcomings,
Uses a pinch of successes
Sprinkles in our understandings.
Adds an ounce of celebrations
Stirs in our health and our illness
And our struggles and bereavements,
Adds a large drop of our weakness.
Blends in our devotion and love,
Includes a few drops of our strife
Adds a cup of our strength and joy,
Weaves a tapestry that's our life.

Agnus Dei

Life's full of decisions to make,
Holy Spirit give us insight.
Reveal to us Your proper way,
Agnus Dei relieve our plight.

A gracious smile we ever need
That will be seen upon our face,
That will reflect the love of God.
Agnus Dei grant us Your grace.

Daily our prayers we lift to Thee
Praising You, seeking forgiveness.
May our being reflect Your love
Agnus Dei, our holiness.

(Agnus Dei : Lamb of God)

Missio Dei

Are you following God's plan for you
Or asking God to approve your plan?
Are you the leader that you follow?
Does your leader have a broader span?

God has placed a call on your life,
The question is, how do you respond?
Have you put the call on your wait list?
Is walking with God part of your brand?

God wants you involved in His work.
God's still saying, come follow Me.
Exciting things the Lord still does do.
Be a part of Missio Dei.

(Missio Dei : mission of God)

God and Us

God reigns and God is in control.
Yield to Him is our only task.
Strength and guidance He will provide
And in His love we get to bask.

God helps keep us on His right path.
God listens to our ev'ry prayer.
God knows about each of our sins.
God's dependable, always there.

Confess our sins and God forgives.
Serve our neighbor and God does smile.
Be God's witness in all we do,
Walk with our friend an extra mile.

His Story

Life's a heavy burden to bear,
We don't have to face it alone.
Christ is there, He lightens our load,
His efforts work, as oft's been shone.

Christ does ever encourage us.
Make Him part of our comfort zone.
Follow His ways, doing what's right,
Through all of this, our life to hone.

In all that we do, Christ should shine,
Christ should get all of the glory.
With Christ we can accomplish much,
In all we do, live His story.

(Written at the Donelson-Hermitage YMCA)

The Call

The call does come so loud and clear,
And for an individual.
That call never has strings attached,
It is only a simple call.

Be sure that when you hear that call
There are contingencies you'll find.
There will be trials and struggles
And blessings that will blow your mind.

A response from you is required.
The call is for you and is free.
It will be a life-changing time
For Jesus calls, come follow Me.

(John 21)

With God

Peace and tranquility do reign
Because the Lord is in control.
God's Spirit is sending blessings
On those who the Lord they extol.

We undertake our daily tasks
Relying on the Lord's guidance.
Progress we are able to make
As with the Lord we daily dance.

Such excitement and such great joy
We experience with the Lord.
Amazing insights God provides
As we delve deep into His Word.

(Written at the Donelson-Hermitage YMCA)

Recall

Temptations daily we do face,
Into our life they just don't fit.
At times we wonder what to do
For it seems all are doing it.

In our own power we face the charge,
We find our strength is not enough.
We fail to heed God's written Word,
For that is where we find our tough.

Christ overcame Satan with words,
That was the start of Satan's fall.
From that example we should learn
God's Word in our heart's for recall.

(Written at the Donelson-Hermitage YMCA)

Sharing

Other's burdens we are to share[1]
And through God's love, it shows we care.
Not that o'er them we would hover,
God's command, love one another.[2]

God will supply all of our need[3]
If our neighbor's cry we do heed.
Good deeds we must ever provide,[4]
For then in us God will abide.[5]

For your burdens, who helps you bear
And then whose burdens do you share?
In whose strength do you become strong?[6]
Bear fruit, it's to Christ we belong.[7]

---

1. Galatians 6:5   5. John 15:4
2. John 13:34   6. Psalm 68:28
3. Philippians 4:19   7. Romans 7:4
4. Titus 3:14

My Source

Jesus, my strength does come from You.
You've brought relief instead of strife.
You've calmed me through all my toil.
You've given me abundant life.

Through all my ways, You are my source.
All my prayers You've graciously heard.
Abundant blessings You do pour
And You do feed me with Your Word.

As long as I do seek Your will
There are many things that get done.
You are so gracious and so kind,
For me, eternal life You've won.

(Written at the Donelson-Hermitage YMCA)

Called

We are called to be a servant.[1]
We are called to provide service.[2]
We're called by God to serve in love.[3]
We are called to be Jesus' friend.[4]
We're called according to God's purpose.[5]
We're called to fellowship with Christ.[6]
We are each called by God in peace.[7]
We are called by God to freedom.[8]
We are called to the peace of Christ.[9]
We're called in sanctification.[10]
We each are called through the gospel.[11]
We are called to eternal life.[12]
We're called with a holy calling.[13]
We each are called a friend of God.[14]
We each are called to be holy.[15]
We are called out of darkness.[16]
We're called into His matchless light.[17]
We're called for the purpose of suff'ring.[18]

We are called to Christ's suffering.[19]
We're called to inherit blessing.[20]
We are called the children of God.[21]
We are called chosen and faithful.[22]

---

1. Mark 9:35
2. John 13:15
3. John 13:34
4. John 15:15
5. Romans 8:28
6. 1 Corinthians 1:9
7. 1 Corinthians 7:15
8. Galatians 5:13
9. Colossians 3:15
10. 1 Thessalonians 4:7
11. 2 Thessalonians 2:14
12. 1 Timothy 6:12
13. 2 Timothy 1:9
14. James 2:23
15. 1 Peter 1:15
16. 1 Peter 2:9
17. 1 Peter 2:9
18. 1 Peter 2:21
19. 1 Peter 2:21
20. 1 Peter 3:9
21. 1 John 3:1
22. Revelation 17:14

Other Books of Poems
By the Author

2023

2023

2023

2024

2025

2012
[out of print]

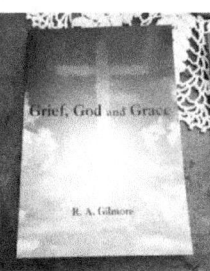

2019
[get from author]

2020 – PDF
[get from author]

www.ingramcontent.com/pod-product-compliance
Lightning Source LLC
Chambersburg PA
CBHW060547260626
47161CB00003B/1088